THE BOOK WHISPERERS

INTRODUCTION

Welcome, a'body! It's so genuinely brilliant to see you here in these times (I tried to find an adjective or two to describe 'these times' but I couldn't. Jings, it must be bad 'cos I'm pretty nerdy wordy!) Anyhoo how did we get here? Well, it's like this ... Mary Turner Thomson, Lea Taylor and I had too much coffee one morning at Dobbies Garden Centre whilst we were squabbling over a sausage. 'Ooooh,' said one of us, can't remember who, 'wouldn't it be a good idea to get a whole load of like-minded folk together so we can help kickstart those books they've been longing to write forever, to share good creative energy and to facilitate encouragement of one another in an uplifting positive way? And how about we do it just because we can and because we want to put good stuff out into the world just now when everything's going to hell in a handcart?'

Well, you can imagine the excitement! More coffee was ordered and in the blink of an eye, the sausage was abandoned and there started not a little swinging from the light fittings, which is not easy in Dobbies.

Susan Cohen, Author

www.TheBookWhisperers.com

Susan Cohen

Mary Turner Thomson

Lea Taylor

Mrs B Matthew
5 Kilmany Road
Gauldry
Newport On
Tay
DD6 8RW

CONTENTS

ALONE

by Mandy O'Connor

'When the outside is frightening and the inside is worse.'

HOLD ON

by Mary Turner Thomson

I called at 8am – the moment their telephone lines opened. I knew I'd have to wait but at least I'd be (one of the) first to get in the system. I wasn't alone.

...

Sorry to keep you waiting, all our lines are busy at the moment. Please hold, and we will answer your call as soon as we can. [Music] ...

...

After an hour of tapping my feet and killing time googling stuff I don't need, I transcend through irritation and start to feel sorry for the telephone operators. They must be so exhausted answering call after call from stressed, irritated and panicking people. I imagine their phones as red hot, and their ears burning.

...

[Music] ... All our lines are still busy please hold and we will answer your call as soon as we can. Or if you prefer, you can call back later. Our opening hours are 8am to 6pm Monday to Friday. [Music] ...

...

After two hours I start to wonder if the person who wrote the hold music – which doesn't change – is actually getting royalties for its performance. If so, they're going to make a LOT of money out of this situation.

...

[Music] ... We are currently experiencing a high volume of calls. If you have an existing face to face appointment booked you must not attend the job centre or continue with this call. We will contact you. You will continue to get your payments but you must report the changes in circumstances. Do this where possible via your online account. Our offices remain open if you need us.

...

After three hours I start to hear an irritation and intonation in the recorded message - as if the person is getting tired of saying it over and over ... and over again. The repeated musical interlude is jangling as I imagine the musicians' fingers starting to sting and bleed. I can hear it in the shards of the grating notes. I can feel madness pressing on my temples - is this a version of Chinese water torture in audible form?

...

If you have made your claim online and are calling to book your first appointment then stay on the line. If you feel you still need to speak to us your call will be answered as soon as possible. Or if you prefer you can call back later. Our opening hours are 8am to 6pm Monday to Friday. [Music]

...

I imagine that I will be here all day. That the phone will run out of charge. That I will have to do the same all over again tomorrow. I accept defeat. I will be doing this for days and days on end because I have no option but to keep holding on. The voice and the music start to sink into the wallpaper as I zone it out.

Then suddenly, after three and a half hours, a very depressed sounding woman answers the phone.

"Hello." She says. The word is dripping with suppressed tension, almost like she was holding back from screaming for hours on end.

"Firstly," I say, "I want to tell you what an amazing job you're doing. Thank you for being there and for helping so many people."

Immediately the woman brightens. "Thank you," she said with almost a sob in her voice.

I try and keep my call as short and efficient as possible for her. My daughter needs her identity verified to be able to claim Universal Credit – having no credit history she can't do this online – and the woman walks us through the process and even makes us a telephone appointment.

At the end of the 5 minute call I thanked her again and said, "Keep doing good work, and even if people sound tired, frustrated or upset when they talk to you, just remember that you are helping them enormously and it is appreciated (even if they don't say it at the time)."

Again she thanked me with soft relief in her now stronger voice, and I wished her a great day.

If nothing else is done today, I have given one stranger a moment of light. It may only be one candle in the dark ... but it is something.

AT THE WOOD'S HEART

by Lea Taylor

Walk with me
beneath boughs
of greening leaves

We will pass
secret places
where fledglings
learn to spread their wings

And wander along the
mossy paths
past the ferns and
fawns hidden

We will dance in
dappled sunlight
At the woods heart
to the song of the forest
Come, walk with me.

INSIDE THE MIND

By Liza Miles

These past days living in isolation have dampened my natural optimism. Random thoughts race through my mind as I search for the unsigned will; who can sign it now? Neither neighbour or close friend. By procrastination I have failed, not made things clear, I will leave a mess if the worst happens.

The thoughts hit me hard, like bricks through a window. I feed the cats, make breakfast and put on some music, but the cloud of gloom clings to me like a veil.

Enough! I jolt myself internally with a boot up the backside, it almost works. I settle for wearing a dress over jammie bottoms and apply lipstick, just in case a virtual meeting is called.

Sitting at the makeshift desk by the window in my bedroom I surprise myself with concentration. The silence of home working, filled only by pings and dings of incoming emails and texts.

It's almost five as I stretch and finish work for the day. A solid seven, I congratulate myself, log-off and activate the radio app on my phone. Usually a news and talk radio junkie since CORVID I have rationed myself to the news twice a day. Its all I can stand, but tonight I can't even bear that and stand in my kitchen yelling at the speaker.

"What do you mean you will, We need to...... Just f'ing get on with it!"

My voice grows louder, harder as inner frustration, fuels fear, and anxiety. I want to be comforted, assured that all is going to be alright, instead, I feel let down, disappointed, hurt. I take a breath and look at my watch?

The bottle of Red Tempranillo beckons, well it is after five, so why not. Maybe dinner and a movie, after a sojourn in my garden. I feel thankful for the outside space, leaving the house with wine and a book, the radio app off.

My isolation reading calls for escape, fleeing from tragedy. But, despite the tempranillo and the sun on my face, my eyes can barely focus on the pages of Billy Connolly, the big man does not inspire laughter today.

I close the book and sit in silence as a big furry bee bumbles her way into the ground, detecting the sweet new shoots making their way through the soil. Her busyness consoles and calms me, and my ears attune to the sounds of the birds filling the sky instead of the usual buzz of traffic.

"Thank you, Bee." Her presence is comforting.

Billy Connolly beckons and this time a loud guffaw lets rip. Morbidity gives way to optimism and hope and I realise this time of Isolation, a brief moment in the history of time, is a small price to pay for tomorrow's to come.

THE CLAP

by Toni Thomson

It's 8pm on Thursday
And I totally forgot
The neighbours all went out to clap
I, well I did not!

At first I felt guilty
Then I felt fine
I didn't clap this evening
But I raised a glass of wine!

Someone made a comment
About me being missed
I smiled and told him politely
I was indoors getting pissed!

Apparently I let them down
They had to stamp their feet
Just to make lots of noise
To beat another street!

I will go out and clap again
Along with those I know
Because I really want to
But Not just for show.

I won't be bashing pots and pans
Or making up a rap
I'll be standing on my doorstep
Giving a thankful clap!

LIKE A TREE

by Liz Thomson

You're like a tree -
you stay still and hardly move.
You say seeds are slow but they grow and change.
You sit there still as a glacier. (And sometimes as cold.)
Staring at a screen. Looking for truth, entertainment or someone
to relate to? Something to keep your interest. You don't want to be like
other people. You want individuality which is understandable. You grow
your farm and mine your stone online. My seeds have grown into small
plants in the ten days since you last went for a walk. They're moving faster
than you. See that you're part of nature - you belong and are loved.
Important, a one-off. I love you and you have friends. The hugs
you're so good at giving. My parenting, I hope
you're forgiving. Want the best for you
now and always.
Maybe you need
this time, to look
at what's next.
We'll miss you
when you've gone
off into the world
to make your
way. Only three
months away.
Please come out and
go for a walk - I'd
enjoy a talk. To see you smile, once in a while and see you grow
and change. However slowly - like a tree you grow tall and strong.
Looking forward to see you become the man that you want to be.

LOST AND FOUND

by Jan Bee Brown

I have lost it. The thief tiptoed in and left quietly. She made off with it mid cough although which cough I cannot recollect.

I know who she is, she knows my flat intimately, she lingers long in my laundry, lurks in my fridge and she rummages through my bins. She lies brazenly amongst the wee free samples in my make-up bag and takes regular continental visits to the litter tray. I imagine her in her laboratory amidst the shelves of brown glass bottles with orange rubber pipets, all neatly labelled: Walk in the Park, Curry Night at the Karma, Kitty Litter - Ammonia Rising. Dressed in her white coat with her grey hair tightly tied in a long plait she bends over her specimen jars creating complex chords.

Balancing high notes with low she composes a symphony of smell. She takes a small brass key from the chain around her neck and opens the box marked 'Precious', inside the small lump of hard mass looks uninteresting unless, like her, you are an aficionado of ambergris. She takes a jar of Joy Juice from the shelf marked 'Simple Pleasures', decants Sweat of Stallion at a social distance then shakes vigorously. She takes a taper and dips it in the heady brew before rocking it rhythmically back and forth under her nose.

She puts her head on one side and purses her lips... something is missing, a hint of Cheap Perfume perhaps? No ... too obvious, Fake Tan? No ... not classy, Chopped Garlic? "Yes!" She purrs with pleasure and adds Squeeze of Lemon. Sun Cream, yes perfect - but which variety? She smiles and whispers "Coconut". She knows she has a lovely pair somewhere, and what an absolute treasure is a Coconut, sealed in its unassuming shell, rough and ready, milky, fleshy.

Madame Covid stole my sense of smell yet still she knows how to press my buttons and trip the switch to trigger a million memories.

Welcome readers to my desert island disco: Mother-milky Breast Dad's Aftershave Sister's Socks Brother's Breath Granny's Gym-bag Granddad's Pipe Dog Paws Pleasured Bed Baby's Head Chips & Vinegar Fried Onions Vicks Vapour Rub And if all but one were washed away by the next cough?

I twist the green cap of the blue glass jar in my hand and rub the balm on my chest. I smell nothing but feel a cool hand on my forehead, catch a flicker of concern suppressed with a smile.

"Night night, sleep tight. Make sure the bugs don't bite."

My chest swells and my skin tingles I hear a door gently shut and my mother's footsteps descending the stair.

LETTER TO AUNTY MADGE

by Lea Taylor

Dear Aunty Madge,

How is the social isolating going? Now, remember, you are in the category where you are not allowed to go out. Not even to put the cat out! I'm so glad you managed to figure out how to Zoom, Skype, Facetime, Messenger and email. We seem to be seeing so much more of each other now don't we? And yes, you did rather catch me unawares at my second breakfast yesterday. I know, still in my nightie at 11am, naughty me. But at least I had changed when I spoke to you again at 2pm.

Of course, you must feel at a loss to know what to do with yourself now that The Archers are off air and all your favourite soaps aren't doing their usual slots. Have you discovered NetFlix at all? I can highly recommend it. Lots of golden oldies there to revel in.

I hope you are remembering to wash your hands after the nice young man delivers your food parcel - to coin your favourite phrase 'cleanliness is next to Godliness.' And please do remember, sensible eating, were not in rationing now you know. Although you did rather worry me when you mentioned boiling up Uncle Jock's old socks to make soup - was that a joke I wonder? Which reminds me, how is the home-made wine coming along? Your singing last night was rather rousing. We could still hear it above the Thursday night clapping. Still, I'm glad to see you enjoying yourself, though I hope you don't mind me saying, do remember to put your teeth in next time.

I managed to get out in the garden again the other day. I had planted some seeds but next door's cat seems to have scratched them up. Such a pity, I was looking forward to having a plot rather like Monty Dons. Never mind though. I'll keep trying. Although I must say, I do seem to have had some success with the tomato plants my nephew gave me. Not a hint of tomato yet but a lovely pungent smell, makes me feel quite giddy.

I took a walk yesterday afternoon but there were so many people on the path it was difficult to keep to the recommended social distancing. I found myself politely dodging from side to side and still ended up bumping into the other walker.

Tesco's now have a policy of only allowing you in to shop if you are wearing a mask. I very nearly turned home this morning but then remembered I had a clean pair of smalls in my pocket, so put those on. Not very pretty with the gusset over my mouth but it did the trick and had a marked effect of people's sense of social distancing too. Marvellous. Isn't it amazing how resourceful we have all become. Yes, Covid19 has been rather unpleasant but there are still many little gems to be found in spite of it all.

Stay safe, stay well and much love,

Your loving niece,

Lea xx

THE NEW NORMAL

by Beverley Webster

Thanking God my boyfriend moved in just before this started
Otherwise we'd be alone, indefinitely parted.
He's set up to work from home, on the end of the dining table
I'm doing jobs around the house, as far as I am able.

We've sorted out the cellar for more room to store his things
And are starting to adjust to all the niggles closeness brings,
The summer house gives us a break when this terraced home feels small
Building it two years ago now proven a bloody good call!

Exercise is mowing the lawn and shearing back the hedges,
Mulching the remnants, composting all and tidying the edges.
I must set up my old Wii fit and play some games, for sure,
When he has cleared his boxes that are stacked up on the floor.

On rare days we go out of doors with shopping list and mask,
Walk to the park to take a stroll, before that daunting task;
The supermarket shop now starts by queuing on taped lines,
Hoping we'll find those rare essentials; toilet rolls and wines.

Cooking's more creative now we can't get our normal brands
And it's frequently disrupted by the need to wash our hands.
Luckily we'd got some grains and cans in our store cupboard
Pasta's scarce and if you need tinned goods at all you're buggered.

Evening choices include quizzes and "recorded live" plays,
Or virtual meetings with your friends on a screen split twenty five ways.
More repeats on tv and the news is full of doom -
Most journalists give updates from their cosy living room.

At times like this we need to find a way to keep us sane,
For me that means I must connect with my creative brain
This poem's only one of several writing tasks I've started
To get on with the rest of them it's time that I departed...

DANCING AND DOWNTON WITH DAD

by Georgia Whitehead

Since Covid-19 struck and we are all stuck in our homes, it is easy to say that activities are becoming increasingly hard to think of, especially with my dad. My dad is a man who can never sit still, so much so his nickname is the Duracell Bunny. The kitchen cupboards have been emptied, cleaned and sorted. The floors have never been so clean and the bathrooms positively glow. Cakes have been baked, new recipes have been tried and the hedges and lawns have been trimmed to within an inch of their lives. Jigsaws completed, quizzes, puzzles and word searches have all fallen to his march on boredom. And this is all in week one. With my dad at the helm of our quarantine ship, things that we could have spun out for months have been achieved in just seven days. So, what to do? My dad refuses to sit and watch Netflix before 5pm so sadly TV is out. There was only one thing left; dancing.

My dad cannot dance. At all. Now I am no Anton du Beke, but he makes Shrek look like Tinkerbelle. With two left feet dancing comes as naturally to my father as walking would to a fish. Spurred on by videos of my brother dancing to 'Thriller' and not to be outdone we embarked on a dancing journey. With 'Shake a Tail Feather' the song of choice, my dad expected to turn into a Blues Brother overnight. We are now on day five of dance rehearsals and sadly he still hasn't made it past the first movement. Walking in a square when put to music seems to send him into a spiral of confusion. We haven't even made it to the 'grapevine' yet he is still envisaging backflips, twists and cartwheels. We have changed the song three times as he blames the music not his feet and now we are back to square one. My mother sits and bangs a pan to help him keep time; all to no avail.

When not dancing, my dad has a new-found interest in Downton Abbey. He hated Downton Abbey before quarantine, however he is now a born-again period drama lover. Instead of discussing the news, we now discuss whether Lady Mary will marry Matthew and the scandal of Sibyl running away with the chauffeur. He frets about Mr Bates, wonders whether Thomas and O'Brien will get away with their plotting, and constantly complains about the expense of the Downton dinners as if he himself was funding them. Now our very own Lord Grantham, he walks the garden, surveying and making grand plans for birdhouses, pizza ovens and more decking. All this dancing and 'running of the estate' tires him out however and he is asleep by 10!

Downton and Dancing has now taken over our lives but the sheer joy that my dad gets from something as simple as this puts a smile on my face every day, despite the circumstances.

WHAT I LEARNED YESTERDAY DURING THE PANICDEMIC (TM)

by Lach

So, I've been watching myself in isolation for several weeks now and I've finally got the courage to do it. I've asked myself out!

I know, I know, crazy right? But it worked, I said yes!

I was so nervous! I'd been thinking about myself for days. I'd catch glances in the mirror, and I was looking right at me! I just felt something was there. We have so much in common. For instance, I like having coffee in the morning, and so do I! We like all the same shows on Netflix, Though I like "The Middle", but I don't think I do. Also, we both like bagels, but I may have a wheat allergy. Still, those are such small things. And I know I shouldn't think this way but I believe that I can change him. I know, I know, baby steps. But I took the first real big one and it worked!

So, we have a date and it's for tonight! OMG, I'm so excited. It's a simple dinner and a movie date, but still why am I so nervous? I've been spending all morning trying to figure out what to wear. It's probably futile because we have such similar tastes. I just know I'll wear the same thing as me. But I'm sure we'll laugh about it.

I'm picking myself up at six and taking me out to dinner in the living room. I'm making a fish dinner in case I'm a vegetarian. (Oh God, please don't let me be a vegan, I can't live without meat altogether!) Anyway, after dinner we'll go to the front room, get comfortable and watch something neither of us has seen before. Probably a Jennifer Aniston romcom to get in the mood. The mood! What am I saying, it's just our first date! OK, ok, tone it down. Maybe a Jen movie is too much? Rats, now I'm panicking! OK, OK, breathe. I'll let him pick the movie and that'll give me a clue to what my intentions for me are. Alright, I better go. I still have so much to do before I see me tonight

Wish us luck!

IN THE BEGINNING

by Betty Skelton

He sat by the window.
She sat by the window.
He smiled.
She frowned.
He sighed.

He sat by the window.
She sat by the window.
He waved.
She looked.
He smiled.
She frowned.
He sighed.

He sat by the window.
She sat by the window.
He waved.
She looked.
He raised one eyebrow.
She wrinkled her nose.
He smiled.
She frowned.
He sighed.

He sat by the window.
She sat by the window.
He waved.
She looked.
He smiled.
She looked away.
He looked down.
She looked back.
He looked up.
She smiled.
He smiled.
They grinned.

STALKED

by Daniel Duggan

The words are stalking me,
in every vennel and side street,
there is an artery of bloody handed,
top hat wearing,
moustache twirling sentences.
The flow of the raincoat,
the doth of that hat,
is a sly gesture,
a shipwreck of a letter,
sent as a heartbeat inside heartbreak.
It's a hand movement,
a fist shaped as a gun,
finger as a trigger,
a knot undone.

JOY

by Liz Thomson

I wrote a children's story but then someone told me that there was one almost identical to it and so, I've stalled on that for the moment.

Recently, we've enjoyed seeing my neighbours young girls, 9 and 6 when I hang the washing out with one or two of our sons (twins who are 20 and an 18 year old).

Our neighbour downstairs has a 5 year old son, who is impressed with one of our older sons tricks on his mountain bike rearing up like he's on a bucking bronco. He came out of his back door in his pyjamas to say hello and waved, then went back indoors. He has a baby sister and brother (twins) who we can hear crying occasionally and sometimes see them smile the most gorgeous smiles when they're in the garden with their parents. Our gardens all back onto each other.

The neighbours children remind me of ours when they were younger with their innocence, enthusiasm for swinging, running and climbing. The girls have just started to play football every morning. Ours used to love that at school and we'd play together as a family. I was a little nervous of being hit in the face with the football but often laughed so much that I couldn't play properly.

I'm trying to do piano again – I'm only grade 1 but it's improving slightly. I'm encouraged by the older girl who practises her piano next door, "Memories" and, "I'm the King of the Swingers" ring through the wall each day. She's better than me.

Went for a walk with my husband and our three sons the other day. At one point our boys (or I should say, young men) shoved and then chased each other like they were children again – laughing and joking. So much energy and fun. The sun was shining and the sky was blue with classic fluffy clouds. It felt like we were a family again and we went on to have some interesting conversations – great to have seen them grow from babies till now and what lovely young people they've become.

That park has been a sanctuary with the trees, the bright yellow gorse flowering and smelling of coconut and vanilla, the cherry blossom, the pond with the ducks chasing each other and the swans. Saw a swan come into land and you could see the white reflection in the water and then the skid on the surface with the water spraying as it landed so gracefully. I even saw a couple of deer alongside the blood moon the other evening – they looked this way and that, twitched their ears and galloped off. My family, my neighbours' children, the natural world and that park has made me feel more connected and appreciative over these past few weeks – just before the lockdown, I realised that being outside is essential for feeling well and happy.

Want to go back to that children's story and put in some of that joy found in nature and childhood

WEE MINNIE'S HEARTBEAT

by Wee Minnie

Help me to make rainbows with my tears,
Help me to make starlight with my fears,
Help me see beyond the years,
And find the courage to overcome,
Walking free in the sound of a
Different drum.

SUNRISE

by Suzy Enoch

I got up at five-thirty. Not because I wanted to, but because my nipple was sore from being chewed on by the baby. Well, not really a baby any more now that he's two, but I'm a continuum concept parent and the baby isn't showing any signs of wanting to stop so we're still going. I made a vat of tea and mused that really I should do some training. If the world ever turns again and my work starts up, which there is no reason to believe it won't, then it would be nice to be fighting fit and ready for it. Grabbing the gigs and feeding my starving bank account. But the world shows no signs of starting up just yet.

I looked out of the kitchen window and the sun was starting to rise over the hills, the first hazy rays of light dawdling down to the tree line and burning off the morning mist. Pink, white, grey, green, yellow and blue, constantly changing. If I have to be shut up anywhere I'm glad it's here, in the middle of nowhere in the middle of beautiful nature.

I shifted slightly moving closer to the window and stepped in cat sick that had a rats head poking out of it. I jumped violently back, stifling the scream that I knew would wake the children, determined to grab every second of precious solitude, even if I was covered in ratty cat sick, but, of course, as I leapt so did my tea tipping itself down my leg. I leapt again, bracing myself for scalding pain, and stepped back into the ratty cat sick, this time skidding just a bit and smearing the gelatinous mess between my toes and across the floor. I regained my balance and stood stock still. Luckily, my dressing gown absorbed the heat of the tea so by the time the liquid touched my skin it was not burning, but merely a bit hot. As a person who is usually cold I momentarily appreciated my warm leg. The rest of my tea was now on the floor since I had dropped the cup with the shock of ratty cat sick experience number two, so I picked it up. I looked at it. Miraculously, it had landed upright and there was still a bit of tea in the bottom.

'Should I?' I thought to myself.

Outside the sky was now in flames as the sun appeared over the horizon, and for a moment I forgot my slimy foot, warm, wet leg and filthy kitchen. There are certain circumstances where waking the partner to look after the kids is justified, even though it is my morning. Extreme disgustingness and danger of toddlers poking regurgitated rats is one of them. But if I started now I could be showered and cleaned just as the children woke. No mummy time, no cup of tea and no rest.

So I stood, drifting into the hills, my mind leaving my contaminated body and wandering into the sunrise. Everything could wait. After all, it's not like we had anywhere to go.

THE WORLDS LIFE

by Leroy-Jay Leslie-Dalley (aged 14)

The moon falls, and the sun rises,
the birds wake, and sing their song.
The people wake, and start their day,
singing in their own way.

The flowers bloom, and the bees buzz,
the trees sway, as the wind blows.
When the Nocturnal animals go to bed,
the non-Nocturnal animals wake, to start their day.

The cars, bikes and trucks, start their engines,
and go about their day, driving people around.
The planes fly, high in the sky, and the boats sail,
down on the sea, fishing and touring.

Schools open, and children work,
listening and learning.
The adults go to to work,
helping people and making their lives better.

The sun goes down, and the moon rises,
letting people know it's time to sleep.
The moon falls, and the sun rises,
telling everyone it's a fresh new day.

Volcanoes erupt, spewing their magma,
turning its surroundings to ash.
Earthquakes rumble, moving land,
buildings topple, and turn to rubble.

Tsunamis rise, and hit the land,
washing everything away.
Hurricanes swirl, leaving destruction,
and chaos in its wake

Coronavirus, terrible
no actual cure,
all we can do is pray, to make it go away

We stay inside
the vehicles stop, the machines end.

The worlds ozone layer get a chance to repair
letting us live, just a little longer.

We can't stop this, nobody can,
because this is the worlds life.

MINE

by Ginny Britton

When you've discovered that moment of rawness
within you that heralds a new awakening.
A freedom that was yours by rights but was taken from you.

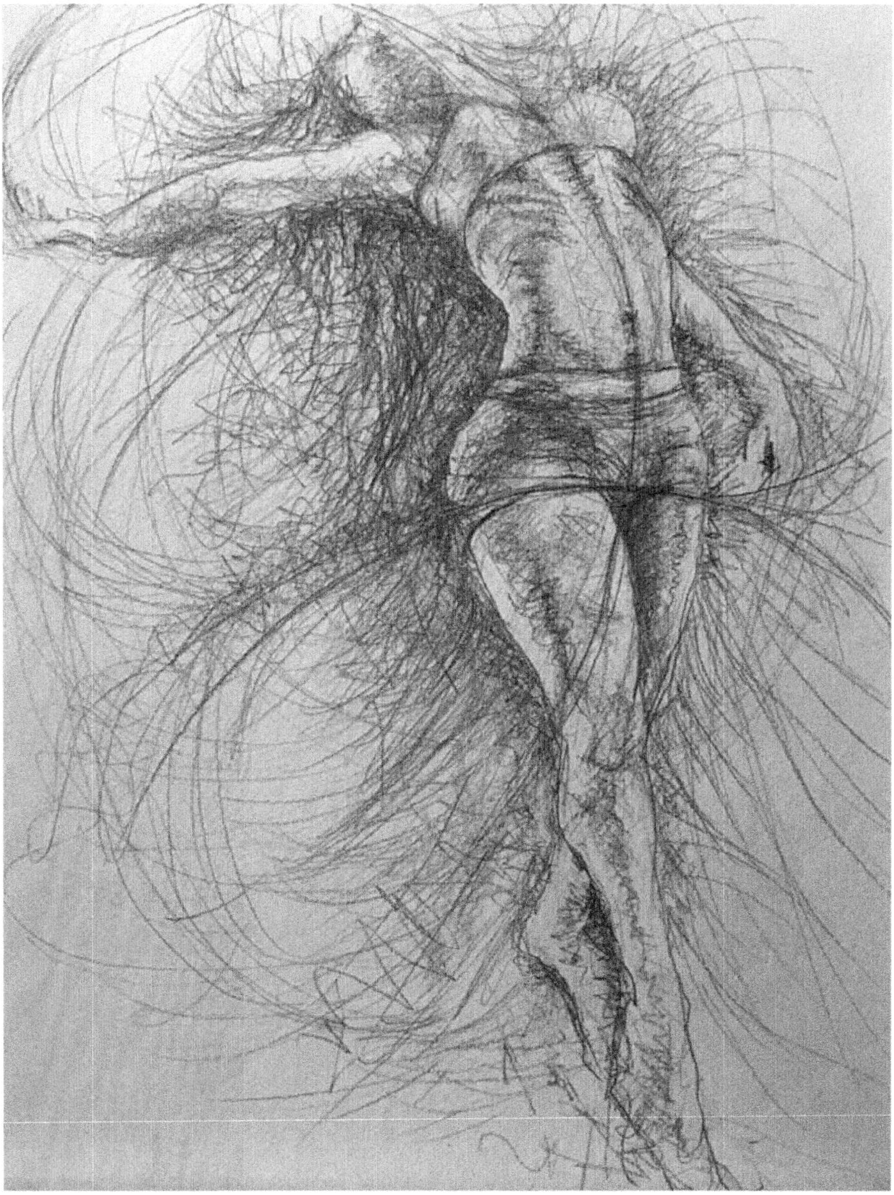

AND IT CAME TO PASS

by Liza Miles

And it came to pass, as the earth dwellers grew quiet, the language of the birds could once again be heard throughout cities.

Father Time and Mother nature looked down from the highest point.

"It is peaceful," said he.

"It was almost all gone," said she.

Together they spread their arms, which were long enough to reach around the world, and embraced each other from the North to the South and from the East to the West.

They both knew the precarious edge on which the world was teetering. The sands had flowed fast, speeding the pendulum close to midnight.

"Have they learned?" he said

"Not yet" she replied quietly.

NO TITLE ...

by Toni Thomson

There they sat
In all their glory
Helping us all to write our own story.

Mary wore tape
Lea had a parrot
Susan a bow I'd like to inherit!

This week it's structure
Plan out the plot
Rewrite and rewrite and rewrite a lot.

A recap on last week.
Plenty of praise
For the writing produced the past seven days.

Carry on writing
The creativity you seek
Could come from the outfits being worn next week!

Thank you ladies.

COCKTAILS

by Suzy Enoch

There once was a mum stuck at home,
Who schooled her three kids on her own,
They were filled with defiance,
'Til cocktails in science,
Now they have a much more mellow tone.

PROOPS PENSIVE PROSE

by Margery Bambrick

Our rituals, beliefs and customs have changed with time. Many forgotten. Many neglected. Even more lost.

They have now taken on other 'dressings' we wear and ways we think are enough.

We have forgotten that tree's are living beings capable of teaching us so much.

We have forgotten how precious the bee's and insect kingdom is and the part they play in the cycles of life.

We have forgotten to be grateful for the beauty of the Earth and all nature brings us.

We have forgotten to listen to nature and Mother Earth. What is she telling us?

Do we listen to the birds, sense the smells of honeysuckle wafting in the breeze, the scent of roses, garden thyme and mint offering from the larder of nature.

Nature in the northern hemisphere is coming back to life and back from its sleep.

We have a chance, an opportunity, to accept new beginnings, new rituals, new ways of being, many going back to the gifts nature has always been handing us and we have turned our back on.

We have the chance to embrace nature more, to embrace each other and to give back in our rituals.

What path will we choose? Back to where we were? Or will our path change.

Meantime I am off with a cuppa to listen to the birds as I ponder on my answers.

SOCIAL DISTANCING STICKS

by Dave Axon

To put this piece into context... This is my reply to an email from my friend in deepest Derbyshire who masquerades under the pen-name of Ackroyd Poskitt, to protect the innocent. Ackroyd had just sent me visual images of Distancing Sticks for separating socialists in the case of a break-out. There were two, each with a pointing hand at one end. The second one was for use in the case of someone creeping up behind. Ackroyd wishes to remain anonymous, if he could only spell it.

Dear Ackroyd,

I was just thinking of sending you a missive, intercontinentally speaking.

Here in Andalucia we have lots of sticks, in fact I have several hundred of the Cane Variety, or is it Mutiny? Still, better than a Stitch In Time, as Stephen Hawking once memed.

Today we have been mostly planting Moringa trees, as Spain is closed, so I can't buy any more garden gnomes from IKEA. We did use several sticks, but in the upright position to provide sport and ward off Corona bottles. The last Moringa tree was tricky as, on the way back from Cómpeta Garden Centre (turn left at Algarrobo), we were harried on the motorway by a passing stranger who indicated a snapped Moringa tree hanging from our borrowed open-plan truck. We duly turned into a Garden Centre with large chairs in the car park, no mean feat for a borrowed truck, priced up a fire pit (1,950€ including storage but no wood in the storage) and treated the injured Moringa with an improvised splinter, made from Moringa wood.

We are now in locks down mode, although for those of us who are follicly challenged, that is quite difficult. Still, we must do our best. So, in the National Interest I am self-prevaricating and this morning I did some garden shredding (half an Acacia, or Aca, as we call it), dug a planting hole with my percussion hammer-drill (Einhell brand - like a Kango but cheaper, and you get a free angle-grinder) and combined compost ingredients in my cement mixer, the must-have gadget when you live in the campo, or Spanish countryside, whichever comes first.

Hang on, says I, this is what I've been doing here since December, 2006 más o menos. I must be side-kick, or pre-affluent. Actually, the Pre-Affluents were a randy bunch of interior decorators who painted Muriels with their locks down. What goes around comes around - and gets dizzy as well.

Keep Karma And Carry On Gardening.

It's a funny old world.

"They laughed at me when I said I was going to be a comedian; they're not laughing now". (Bob Monkhouse, 1972).

Rearguards,

Dave

I’M IN!

by Kate Trought

It’s the rona, mate..
Gotta isolate.
Stay indoors
Do the chores
Try to not gain weight.

It’s the rona, mate...
Gotta wear a mask
Keep a distance
Seek assistance
Though I hate to ask

It’s the rona, mate...
It really is a pain
But I’m so old
Must do as I’m told
But it goes against the grain

It’s the rona, mate....
So there is no better time
To sit right down In my dressing gown
And write a rubbish rhyme

TRUE STORY ...

by Tiffany Stephens

In 2014 I attended the New Story Summit at Findhorn. The essence of the week long event was to explore creating a New Story for the world.

On the penultimate day several boards bore many post it notes related to the workshops and side groups that would be participated in the following day.

The next morning we all assembled in the Universal Hall. On the boards the post it notes had been rearranged into the words ' We Don't Know'.....

The response to this disruption of order was incredible, verging on hysteria for some. Chaos was at play. What people had anticipated and put in place was no more. The organisers were dumbfounded.

Some people applauded. Some people broke down, they could not cope. Some people tried to rearrange the post it notes to how it had been before. Some people were despondent and felt they could no longer participate. Some sat and meditated in the midst of the chaos. The 'culprits' were requested to reveal themselves

This is a medicine story...a reflection of humanity's response to change, to disorder, to chaos, to the discomfort of 'We Don't Know'.

I have to say this was the best experience of the whole week for me. To observe the reactions was an insight into people's readiness to change especially considering the intention of the summit.

I share this as I feel it reflects what we are experiencing right now. Life has changed beyond recognition in a short space of time.

Will the 'conspiracy theories' become reality? Is this nature retaliating against human imbalance? Will things return to 'normal'? Etc Quite simply.....'We Don't Know'

Is this an opportunity for change? If so, what would you like the New Story to be?........

BOXED IN

by Mandy O'Connor

Boxed In ...

LOCKDOWN

by Juliette Enoch-Wambergue (aged 11)

I'm stuck in my house, it's too small,
So, I got a new phone to call,
All of my family,
Bob, Rob and Amalie,
But Gran can't use phones well at all!

ISOLATION SELF-CARE

by Toni Thomson

Knickers, knickers, knickers
Wear them if you want
But as I'm isolating
I just don't see the point.
No one's going to pop in
Delivery men stand back
Who will even notice
Will anyone keep track?

Knickers, knickers, knickers
Mine are nice and clean
Dried on the washing line
That's the last time they were seen.
Now folded neatly in a row
Tucked inside my drawers
Ready and walting to be used
If I should have a cause.

Bras, bras, bras,
Underwired or not
Even in isolation
I can honestly report
That these are always useful
Although some people scoff
But when the evening meal is done...
Enough's enough it's off!

Undies, undies, undies
Yes they have a use
And when you're socialising
Isn't that the truth.
But I'm in isolation
I'm caring for myself
My comfort is important
And so's my mental health.

So this is the dilemma
When we get up each day
Do we grab our lovely undies
Or leave them packed away?
Well, I don't care what others say
Or indeed if anyone sees
As I'm in isolation
I'll do just what I please!

AS CORONAVIRUS APPROACHES
by Rosie Mapplebeck

So heres your choice: listen to my voice
Worry yourself into a early grave
or learn to love and trust, be brave
This virus comes to us as a test
Are you "all for one, never mind the rest"
Do you rush out in panic and then bulk buy
poking your neighbouring folk in the eye?
Deprive babes of milk or men of their meat
while you make future profit out on the street?
or step back and reflect upon what you have
What else you can use (newspaper for the lav)
or use leaves from the plants near you in the park
which you go to quietly in cover of dark
keeping your statutory distance from others
the grandmas and grandpas and the nursing mothers
decreed of high risk and advised to stay in
pulling hair out in boredom, ain't it a sin?
Remember the old days, no single use wipes
but hankies and rags, water drawn from the pipes
not taken from mountains, make bleach up if you need
use it fresh over surfaces when you drink and feed
Wash hands with a friction and soap to kill bugs
salve your skin, don't use excessive chemical 'hugs'
Uplift your spirits with beauty and joy
use the Net, use your eyes, take a walk, watch what flies
when the planes cannot move there is peace in the skies
and less carbon dioxide to poison the planet
thats a positive change for good so don't can it
Lets welcome the rest from commuting and office
the 9-5 routines which is where the cough is
Feed a cold, starve a fever, let viruses quiver
weaken distribution while sufferers quiver
alone in withdrawal with neighbours to feed them

Recovered, they rise, immune or carrying seed on
(We will use isolation to publicly free them)
in time it will mutate or not be so virulent
lessen the impact and serious intent
So put on some music and dance out your tension
free up your breathing, make love your intention
Make care your first action, be mindful and present
address all your needs and be sure to be pleasant
for life is a gamble, we win and we lose some
Keep safe, spread the joy, be healthy and wholesome
Keep calm every day, find what gives you pleasure
and we will survive, live and thrive, find our treasure
What matter's our health in our bodies and minds
so be careful and gentle, above all be kind.

EVER-SO-SLIGHTLY SID

by Kate Trought

Ever-so-Slightly-Sid you'll agree
Only did things by halves you see
He'd only ever-so-slightly worked
The rest of the time he'd vaguely shirked
And ignored all the moans from his folks and his mates
About getting a job and going on dates

But one morning he awoke with a jolt
And jumped out of bed. It was nearly a vault
His mind was made up, he'd made a decision
He'd go to the Job Centre- get a position
Just as soon as he'd had a little more sleep
And his bed was inviting, the decision could keep.

Then unknown to him his Mum wrote off for a post
She'd read just the thing while she was eating her toast
She wrote it out fast, said she was Sid
She made up his CV, said what he did
But left out that he'd never been employed and more
He was right for this job. Of that she was sure

Ever-so-Slightly walked into town
Bearing the most enormous frown
He'd had in the post a threatening letter
Saying they had a job and that he'd better
Come for an interview down in the city
No wonder he was feeling a weeny bit jitty.

He'd got up at dawn then got back into bed
Pulled up the covers, pillow over his head
But the alarm pulled him out of his wonderful dream
And now here he was and how he could scream
His hair sticking up all over the place
His shirt was too tight like the grin on his face.

His collar was ever-so-slightly tatty
And so were his cuffs but he'd never been natty
His shoes were all scuffed and down at the heel
But give him a break. His teeth were real!
He pushed up his glasses, adjusted his tie
And took a deep breath. It was do or die.

Ever-so-Slightly pushed open the door
And entered the brightness of brand new decor.
The blonde at the desk gave a huge double take
And stood up offering her slim hand to shake.
Ever-so-Slightly stared at her bug eyed
And felt every ounce of his confidence slide.

But he proffered his hand and took up a stance
He knew this was right. This was his chance
To prove to the world that Sid with and 'S'
Had what it took to not make a mess.
She smiled and she showed him into the den
Of the gloom and the cigar smoke of the world of ad men

They gazed at him squinting, and asked him to turn
They prodded and poked and said they'd adjourn
To chat about whether he was right for this job
But Sid was quite upbeat, he knew that he'd score
In an ad campaign where he was the 'before'.

FEAR ... AND FIGHTING THAT

by Ginny Britton

When your safety is compromised and you fight for your own self worth, but you know someone else has a handle on that. It's the birds in your chest that want to fight it. They'll speak out before your brain has kicked into gear. But you know you they'll fail and fall back into you because that's their safety as much as it is yours.

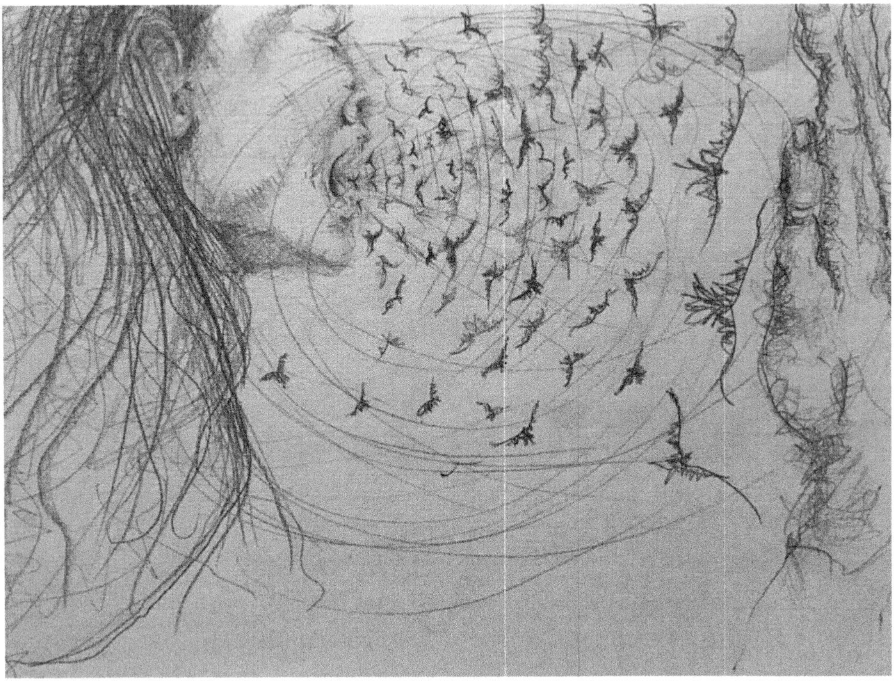

COFFEE SHOP

by Kate Trought

I'll liquefy, stupefy ...
If he comes by.
Sigh.
Oh! Look!
There he is! There he is! There he is!

Where?

There! There!
Over there! Look!

Who? Him?

Yes...Sssh! Don't look!

But ...

Don't look! Sssh!
Do something! Do something!
Stir your coffee...

But ...

What's he doing now? Where is he?
Has he seen me? Is he looking?
Where is he?

He's coming over.

What? Oh no!
Does my hair look all right?

Don't panic. Only a joke ...

A joke? Don't joke. It's not a joke.
Do you think it's a joke?
I'm a joke?

No, Jeez. Chill.

I will. I will.
What's he doing now?
Don't you think he's gorgeous?

Ummm ...

No, don't look. Talk to me
Talk to me. Say something.

Like what?

Anything. I don't know. Anything.
Act normal.
I'm agitated. Heart sated.

He's over rated.

What?
I'm all pulsated
'Cos he came by.
Oh my ...

Sigh

COVID CHRONICLES

by Liza Miles

Ah, Mum, I've dug out the spot for the wildflower meadow but it looks like you are going to have to spend a few more weeks in the blue box. We had it all planned for your birthday on May eighteenth. Safia and I in the garden and Hanaa via facetime. I was going to paint and decorate the half whisky barrel, fill it with fresh dirt, a wee tipple of your favourite Drambuie the hybrid yellow rose At Peace, and your good self. But of course, I didn't purchase the barrel or the rose in time, but who knew that this would be our Spring?

I wonder what you would have made of what is happening now mum, all of us in lockdown and keeping our distance. In fact, I think I can hear you in the kitchen making scones and telling us all to just put our shoulders to the wheel and stop whining and complaining. Folks have had to go through much worse.

I know you did, as a girl educated in an air raid shelter, living through the blitz and the house at the top of the road bombed, the one where your friend lived.

We don't have to live on the sort of rationing you grew up with. But perhaps the fear that today or tomorrow this just might be the last for a friend or a neighbour or someone I know. Well, sadly that's already happened, she was the same age as me too.

I think you would be proud of how we are managing, but it's days like today that I realise how much I miss you. Funny that for so many years we didn't get along, but after I became a mum, well it changed things. You changed too, being a grandmother suited you in the way that being a mum hadn't really. There's a generation, your generation who we are losing because of this virus, this invisible sneaky enemy taking good people, doctors, nurses, care home workers, even some children.

But there are some good things too, the air is clearer, there is more birdsong and wildlife, oh the wildlife, what joy to see pictures of cows on beaches and bears peering in windows wondering where we all are.

I wrote a wee poem when it all first happened. Reading it now it's not very optimistic, but I do hope that we have learned. So cheers mum, thanks for taking a moment to listen to me, I know that you understand.

DECOMPOSING

by Dave Axon

I have several bins
Upon the ground.
Around the house,
They can be found.

Some are large;
Others small
One particular
Is very tall.

In them I put
All sorts of stuff,
Then add water;
That's enough.

Tea leaves, weeds,
Anything goes
Into those bins,
So don't get close.

Or you might find
A different view
When upside down,
Just showing a shoe.

Obsessed am I?
It isn't true.
It's just a phase
I'm going through.

But garden gnomes,
There are a few.
In fact a cull
Is overdue.

There was one
Ugly gnome,
Placed in a tree
And left alone.

But one day
He disappeared.
Never seen again,
It was quite weird.

Who would take
Such a creature,
No use for
A garden feature?

Still we are
Of many hues.
And one man's gloves
Are another man's shoes.

Now this pome
Is getting silly:
Words are pouring
Willy-nilly.

So with your perm,
I will desist.
And go back to
The point I missed.

Which is, if you try
To read this prose,
The words will start
To decompose...

PLATFORM

by Kate Trought

Sooted motes tinge the air
Sulphur billows lift my hair
Heavy, heaving.
Sigh. He's leaving.

Hissing monster squatting steaming
Pressed and ready buttons gleaming
Whistle blowing
Yes. He's going.

Bravely waving, bright eyes blurry
Hankies ready, voices slurry
Fateful clunking of the door
My beloved's gone to war

THE RAILWAY FROM A PAINTING OF THE SAME NAME BY EDUARD MANET

by Kate Trought

But you wrote that you'd be here!
Today, now... here!
Here.
Where we said goodbye.

Look! It says so in the diary I found
After you left
Exactly six years ago.
It said you would always love me
But you had to go.

Look! Just here at the bottom of the page.
Is that smudge one of your tears?
Or mine?

I've dreamed of this moment over many lonely nights.
Dog eared diary under my pillow.
Did you mean all the things you said to me?
Did you mean any of it?
Any of it?

I'm here now,
Waiting.
Like you knew I would.

The train whistles behind me and the steam hisses
The smell of wet coal seems so far away.

Nicolette insisted that we bring the new puppy to show
you.
You.

I don't think I'll wait much longer.
It's getting cold and Nicolette only has a dress on.

It's her best dress.

She wanted to wear it especially to meet her Daddy
For the first time.

VOID

by Malcolm Scott

My life is a bubble right now. Communicating with each other like a nation of Max Headrooms; dissecting the minutiae of the day with our dearest and now not-so-nearest; staying in is the new .going out.

Life lived through the prism of tablets, PCs and mobile devices, punctuated by family quizzes and virtual gatherings.

Weekly bridge meetings and choir practice conducted in fragmented conviviality. The connection gives out and we sing to the wall.

"Ring a ring o' Roses" goes the fatalist vignette sung in innocence by children down the years; revisited, it's a dystopian lament to this creeping pestilence among us.

"Use your time gainfully", say the self-help experts. Pick up your guitar again. Learn Spanish in a week. Get fit. Write that novel!

I try; but procrastination is not my friend, and it too, lurks in the shadows. It steals my time, dashes my hopes, compounds my insecurities.

If only I'd went to university, packed that job in I hated, liberated myself from that corrosive relationship, it would all have been different, wouldn't it?

This new-found spare time lets the mind wander and memories invade and occupy the space, squatting, unwelcome.

I watch yet another formulaic crime-drama box set. One of the actors stirs a negative memory of a late relative; an unresolved argument, a manifestation of theirs, and our own character flaws.

It riles me, the thought endures and lingers; a malign by-product of the recollection.

The abstinence vow is broken; alcohol breaks the tedium and prolongs the day, but the fitful sleep and the late rise the next morning feeds the lethargy, and the day and the evening meld into one...

The chattering classes speak of an "exit strategy". Meantime, we clap our hands and we donate to charity; the previously "unskilled workers" are our new heroes and the political slogans prevail; a white noise of vacuous soundbites.

Salvation seems elusive; we persevere in hope but the expectation is unclear.

We try, we try.

MISSING
by Betty Skelton

I miss...
- visits to the theatre for concerts and for dance
- wanders around galleries to study or just to glance
- ice-cream from the cafe after a long and healthy walk
- setting out the tea and cake for friends to come and talk
- choosing my own shopping -be it milk or bread or jam
- feeling in control with that safety net of calm
- buying tickets for the train to places near and far
- hugs with my children- seeing for myself how they are
- stopping just to blether with folk I meet outside
- that sense of naughty fun with my bus pass 'free' ride
I have missed a last goodbye as they were sent to rest
And snuggles with the newly born ...those cuddles are the best.
I miss knowing that it is safe to venture out the door
I am waiting for the day that we can all do that once more.

WHY

by C E Marshall

Why am I sitting here at home
Alone?
Where are my friends who said they would feed me?
I've been with them whenever they're needy.
No one to talk to,
No one to listen,
Silence is golden,
Except when it deafens.
The reason it seems is something quite nasty,

Come from abroad to infect our whole nation
Ordinary people now in isolation.
Robbed of their freedom to roam at their will.
Out of their depth with the things they must do.
No contact with anyone, that is the rule.
Awake up and listen call from beyond
Violence solves nothing just stay at home
Inside is safe and where you should be
Resting if elderly, working if not.
Under the rooftops is where you must hide.
So when it's over you will have survived.

LONELY LOCKDOWN

by Rosie Mapplebeck

Lonely lockdown Is this how we value our elderly and frail?
We bid them self-isolate, lock themselves away
From any human interaction, care is minimised
Stay at home and bake, but don't share
Your cake, anything you make, sit by radio or tv
Listen to the death numbers rise
Be sure your time will soon come and alone
Phone your children, your friends, attend
To our broadcasts to keep you safe - inside
Where you hide, afraid of the unknown
A virus from which theres no resuscitation
We have no inclination to waste resources
On the non-socially productive.
You must seal
Away from requiring help, our respiratory hell
Of seven day withdrawal of which we complain
While consigning you to three months' soft labour safe from rain
Or any variant of weather or of mood
Locked away in dim rooms in an urban gloom
Do we notice how some stalwart adults now have disappeared?
My vet is over seventy and he's never been feart
But its hard to do your job when the streets have all been cleared
Consultations on the phone work when your clients speak
Not so much when he is a breathless little Peke
So sit tight, dream on, tolerate meagre fare that comes
Its not much better at the shops, affecting everyone.

SAFE

by Ginny Britton

When all you want to do is to run,
but the stillness of a safe place
hold's you tight.

THE BARD O' RATHO STATION

by Malcolm Scott

There was a young man from near Ratho Station
Who penned rhymes for amusement; while in isolation
His old neighbour would cry: "The end it is nigh",
But undeterred, he scribbled, and foist them on the nation.

The print houses they clamoured to publish;
Which surprised him (because he thought they were rubbish),
His mother was proud "my son's a poet", she'd shout loud,
While his father grizzled; and plotted his come-uppish.

They sold in their millions, and the bright lights they beckoned,
"I wrote as I was bored, not for money!" (He reckoned.)
He scrawled some more, until his mind it wizened;
His star waned, the prose withered; the phone deadened.

He didn't seek fame, 'twas a fickle mistress
His books were remaindered, long before Christmas...
Anonymity called, his final destination;
The poor humble wordsmith, from near Ratho Station.

MISCHIEF MAKER

by Shusha Lamoon

Sunday 5th April

Well, what a week that turned out to be! It turns out that you can cause quite a bit of mischief even when you are living on your own and self-isolating. Now, in my condition, supposedly I'm considered "vulnerable" but I wholeheartedly reject that label. I prefer to describe myself as impish or playful, or as my colleagues have been known to describe me, a mischief maker! Monday saw me setting up my new "home office" (read makeshift desk in the corner of the living room) and testing out rather dodgy technology contemplating, as I did, a few ideas as to how I could "structure" my week. On Tuesday morning, before my first Zoom meeting with colleagues, I turned all the books on my bookshelf upside down. Hugely disappointed that no-one noticed, on Wednesday's call, I put my clothes on inside out. Well, that set the tone for the rest of the week! On Thursday, when my neighbours' boys dropped by and left some groceries at my door, I was waiting for them in the window like a shop mannequin. The only costume I could cobble together was a pirate's (using a couple of tea towels, huge gold hoop earrings and a stripey t-shirt). I, rather ingeniously I thought, created an eye patch using black eyeliner. Coincidentally, the dustbin men arrived at the same time so I gave them a pirate wink and an "Ahoy, me hearties!". Honestly, I'm not sure who was most embarrassed but I was in for a penny, in for a pound by this stage. On Friday, when my lovely friend Stella dropped round with my prescription, I serenaded her with a tuneful version of "Isn't She Lovely" from the upstairs bedroom window that Stevie Wonder would have been proud of. As she pulled off the drive, she shouted from the car that I should be certified! And today – today, was just joyous! In the fridge, I had a stack of little chocolate eggs for my grandkids who should have been visiting for the weekend. Just after lunch, I could hear the boys next door playing in the garden. I grabbed the eggs and lobbed them one at a time over the fence without warning. They couldn't work out where they were coming from to begin with. It couldn't have made me any happier to hear their screams of delight and joy as it was "raining chocolate eggs". Having set the bar, I'm really not sure how I can raise it next week, but I'm sure going to have a damn good go!

LOCKDOWN? NEVER IN A MONTH OF SUNDAYS!

by Lesley O'Brien

'I don't think you can freeze wine,' says the woman next to me on her phone, frantically scanning the alcohol section in Tesco's. I shake my head, bemused at the craziness the Corona virus has brought upon humanity. I seem to have been 'lost in action' in these aisles, for a ridiculous amount of time. Having made the mistake of trying to do my mum's and my weekly shop simultaneously, I am suddenly further hindered by a chance meeting with an old neighbour (albeit her intention was good). She whispered that she had it from a good source, that as of 5pm tomorrow, we will be in 'lockdown'. Agh! Cue high pitched screeching 'Psycho' strings. I was now for sure, unable to do my usual, quick as a fiddler's elbow, in and out of the aisles, weekly shop. The further implications of a 'lockdown' were yet to be considered.

Faced with empty shelves, staring at me petulantly, daring me to buy something other than my mum's usual carrot and potato, I stare at the lone asparagus. Asparagus? Asparagus! 'AspAragus,' as my mum had first pronounced it as a child. I now wander, like a lost child up and down the same aisles. No tins of tomatoes, no pasta.

'Tinned meat?' I ask the assistant (my mum was getting a tin of corned beef, whether she had, 'gone off it' or not).

He points and calls, 'Good luck', as if waving me off on some ill-fated voyage to the Antarctic. All around my fellow shoppers appear dazed, like Stepford Wives, whose program has malfunctioned, their mission deleted, as they wander zigidy-zagedy across the Supermarket floor.

The cashier is wearing plastic gloves, she shows me how her Barbie pink pointy nails have pierced a hole. I tell her a joke I saw on Facebook; man wearing a plastic collar, the type usually worn by dogs after an operation.

The dog is saying, 'Noo, it's fur yer ain good. Nae scratchin!'

I tell her, 'My mum's not gonna like the 'nae tatties' report'. As far as my mum's concerned, a dinner without tatties, 'Jist disnae bare thinkin aboot'.

The cashier whispers, (whispering seems to have become a thing), 'A woman yisterday, tried to buy twenty bags o potatoes and then another yin, thirty bottles o wine'.

I recall having a wee joke with the same assistant only a week ago, about the loo roll panic buying. I'd jested we'd just have to cut up The Beano, the way my mum says she used to, during the war. A friend later proudly posted a photo on Facebook of her cyclamen pink towel, neatly cut into strips, ready, present, and correct for re-cycling duty.

I go for a walk later, by the Clyde, best stretch my legs, whilst I've got the chance. Folks are on their verandas on the posh penthouses by the river, watering their plants, opening windows, carrying out 'normal', spring like behaviour. A young woman points her camera at the Charles Rennie Mackintosh mural above The Clutha. I notice the beauty of the picture, framed, by the green of a Scot's pine and the swimming pool blue sky and I fall in love (again) with Charles, the Weggie demi-god. The painting, like an old black and white photo, looking as if he's about to speak and offer a titbit of 19th century wisdom to the bewildered, below.

Two fathers and their children picnic on the grass, blanket and flask strewn aside. One of the boys points to something on the other side of the river, the father listens then patiently explains. Sweet, I think, such a positive scene of dads parenting their kids, yet tinged with sadness that it's still an unusual sight in the 21st century. I can remember only one similar scenario with my dad, camping at Loch Lomond. It was such a wash out, waking up to puddles in the tent, it put me off camping, for twenty years.

Couples are holding hands, chatting, on romantic walks. The treadmill has been taken down a gear. Deadlines lost, people are looking around, taking photos, having picnics. A mindful revolution? But there's always the worriers, who wake up in the middle of the night. Could it be me, my mum, my partner, who'll be struck dead by the virus? Mustn't touch your face. We touch our face over four hundred times a day, a new fact, stored in our already overloaded brains. New worries, are suddenly ubiquitous. Don't touch the bannister, the light switch, the door knob, the petrol pump, the virus could be anywhere!

Twenty-four hours and another Government announcement, schools closed until autumn! Five months! And to beat that, no pubs, clubs, gyms, restaurants or music venues to help keep us sane. No legal lock down yet, but laws are speeding their way through the legal corridors of Westminster and Edinburgh. Boris 'telling' us and Nicola, 'asking' us to 'socially isolate'. A brand new, Orwellian style term, that now rolls familiarly from our tongues. Pupils, parents, teachers are in tears. Society is in shock.

I go for another walk, inspired by increasing fear of a legal lock down. My local park is busier than yesterday. Groups of adolescents at a loose end, one boy, around twelve years old, shakes a padlock and chain, like a prisoner on meltdown.

'Whit are ye looking at? Whit are YOU looking at?'. He rages, adrenalin pumping round his baby face.

'Spare any change?' slurs another youth, in grey joggers and canary yellow baseball cap, eyes red and unfocused.

It's only been one hour since schools out for summer, and it's hardly spring and two hours since Nicola's address to the nation, signs are not looking good. On the other hand, ever the optimist, at least for now, I'm sure I've seen more men, in the last few days, pushing prams, than I've ever seen before. I am hopeful that this could be the beginnings of a giant hurl forward for humankind. As if, to confirm my fledgling hope, Barny has made the dinner, the first in ages, breakfast two days running and is threatening to put the new toilet seat on, I bought months ago. Surely, if everyone is at home, the burden of house-work will ease for women as that ancient excuse, wheeled out for centuries that men are the bread-makers and women the homemakers, clearly is an anachronism... if the virus, cabin fever, suicide or domestic violence, doesn't kill us first? Another game of Scrabble, anyone, anyone...is Skype Scrabble now a thing?

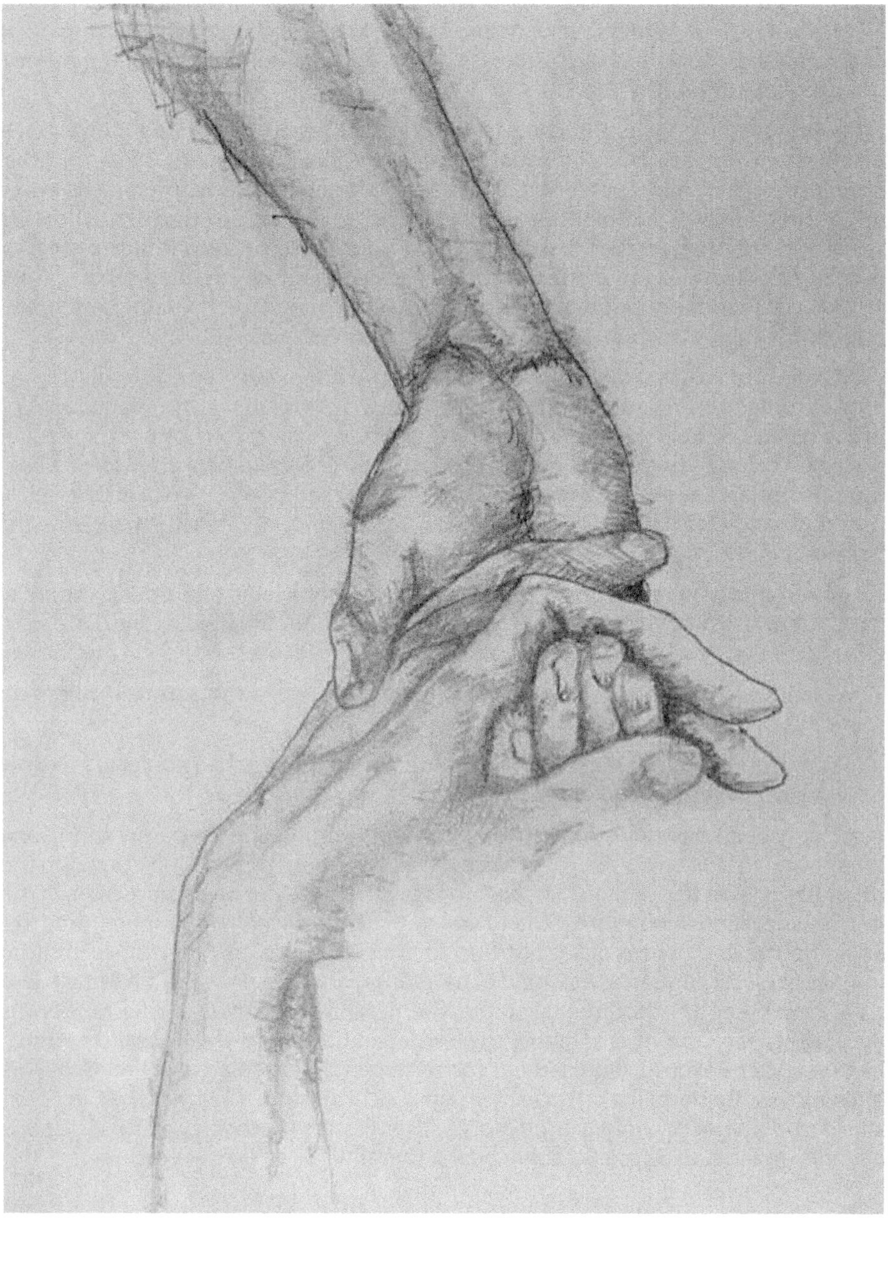

ANCHOR

by Ginny Britton

Even in the darkest of times there is always someone to pull you into the light....

.......If you let them.......

And help is sometimes the bravest word to say....

DEEP WITHIN THE MOUNTAIN

by C E Marshall

Deep within the mountain something stirred. It had been still and dormant since before the mountain formed. Once, it lay upon the ocean floor, hardly moving, taking nourishment from all that was around. It lived a lonely life, just on its own with no knowledge of other creatures that may have been around. Staying still it fed until it grew too large to remain as one and split itself in two. Soon the two became four, then eight, sixteen, thirty two, sixty four, one hundred twenty eight. After four more divisions there were thousands on the ocean floor, and still they multiplied.

When millions made a soup another creature came along and found them good to eat. It could have been the end of them, except, they made a change and instead of food a poison they became and multiplied once more.

The cycle was repeated; many creatures grew in size and they too ate our friend for he had also grown quite large. At each new threat our little friend, he knew just what to do and made his countermeasures to be sure he would survive.

One day the ocean floor did heave and sand and debris upwards went, and with them went our friend. He was among the first to fall back to the ocean floor, then all the rest came down and covered him, he could not move at all. There he lay unseen, unknown, asleep for countless ages.

When the ocean floor heaved up once again, he was unaware, and rose within the rock above the ocean surface. The rock heaved and pushed up, the ocean fell away, our friend was now above the ground and deep within a mountain.

All is dark and all is quiet, so slumbers still our friend. There he would still be if, when the mountain formed, it hadn't taken with it gold. He did not know that it was gold that held him in, he didn't care and slumbered on. But things outside were changing; new animals emerged from forests deep and green. One became an upright creature, intelligent and smart. It found some gold and liked it and came to worship it. The more gold it had the more the creature wanted; greed drove it as a stream does drive the water wheel.

The mountain thought that it was safe, high and lofty, with steep and rugged sides, and so it was, until the creature, man, came up its sides and found the gold and then began to drill. At first our friend felt nothing, then a small vibration before, so suddenly his world did shake and he was in the light with moisture all around. Our friend swelled up and came alive and felt about for food. Gold was not his medium, on it he could not survive.

A softer surface the brushed past and took him from the gold, but it was dry and unattractive, not a surface or which he could survive. Then the light disappeared and now he was surrounded by moisture and warm air flowed over him.

He waited then his chance and used the airflow to take him deep within where familiar darkness encompassed him, and he began to feed.

So the cycle started once again as one became two, two became four until there was soon a soup. The airflow stopped and then the warmth, soon the moisture dried up until at last a fiery flame consumed our friend.

Still his task was not complete, for some of those he had created had escaped in a great gush of air and found another place of moisture warmth and air.

No matter what was thrown at them, our friend's descendants changed and survived. Not so their source of life and when the last source of life died his descendants fell to the ground and once again slumbered until their time should come again.

LOOKING DOWN OR HOW COTTESWOLDE CELEBRATED THEIR FIRST PUBLICKE HOLEYDAY

by Liam Sean McKnight

Deeble woke up, stretched his arms and pulled back the curtains from the window before jumping out of bed.

' What a wonderful day,' he thought, 'the sun is bright the birds are singing and my back ain't aching.'

He walked through the hall to the kitchen; 'Boiled eggs on toast I think but first a cup of tea.'

He went to the front step to get his usual pint of gold-top that Old Farmer Tom had his young son drop off for him each morning.

He opened the door and bent to pick the bottle up from his doorstep and was on his way back inside when something tugging at the back of his mind made him turn around.

'Aah!' he cried almost dropping the milk to the floor. He placed the bottle on the table reserved for his post and walked back out of the door.

He bent over and looked down, 'No,' he thought,' no doubt at all. Some bastards put a hole in front of my door without so much as a by-your-leave.'

He shouted across the street, 'Oi! Nobby! You come out here this minute and tell me what's happening.'

Curtains twitched up and down the cul-de-sac. Folks round here didn't appreciate being woken up at the unseemly hour of nine in the morning by a body a-shouting and a-hollering.

Nobby, appeared at his doorway blinking and yawning in his blue-striped nightgown and his night cap with its yellow pom-pom.

'What be you doing shouting up the whole town Deeble? Ain't heard this much of a racket since somebody put a dead cat in Gramma Gummins post box and she fell back so hard on her fundament that she broke her tail bone.'

'Come here and see for yourself you daft old fool.'

By this time doors up and down the row were filling with people whose interrupted sleep was rapidly being forgotten as they spied an opportunity for seeing something unusual happen. This usually meant one of two things – an almighty stramash or something that would give rise to merriment such as would have the tongues of gossips wagging for months at the snug in The Jug-Eared Farmer.

Nobby crossed the street and looked down too.

'Well, what do that be then?' he asked, removing his night cap and scratching the top of his bald head.

'Buggered if I know. It weren't there last night and it couldn't have been there this morning because Old Tom's son left the milk on me doorstep.'

Just then they both heard a sound that sounded like a voice calling for help from a great distance but before they could deal with that Old Tom came waddling down the street; judging by the colour of his face, some might call it cerise but it was really more puce or even mahogany, no matter, whatever shade it was it was the only way of knowing that Tom was doing the best imitation he could of somebody running.

'Hello Nobby, Deeble. Have either of you seen my boy Jep? He hasn't come back from making his rounds and it's time for taking the herd up to the pasture by the river.'

'Come here Tom and look at this.'

Tom joined Nobby outside Deeble's door. He looked down.

' Well don't that beat all. What'd do that for then Deeble?'

'Me? You daft ha'p'orth. Why would I be doing that and outside my very own door? It were there this morning when I came out to get the milk for me morning cup of tea.'

'Well I gotta go find my lazy no-good son. If you see him tell him he's up far a visit from the front of my hand and probably the back as well.'

Tom looked down, shook his head and went on his way.

By this time almost the whole village was approaching, some of them still pulling on their shirts, dresses, shoes and hats. By the time they had all congregated the only person who wasn't at the scene was the missing Jep and his old man.

Deeble thought he heard the distant call again and this time it sounded like it was coming from below.

'Will everybody please shut up for a minute I think there's something calling from down there.'

'Well that's a fine way to speak to your elders,' said old Elsie to Maisie.

'Yes, not so much as a please ,' agreed Ethel, 'if my old Bert was still here he'd give him a clip round the ear no matter his age.'

Cicely joined in, 'I remember his old mum, Dotty, gods rest her, she brought her boys up to be so much better than this. Never hear Jockle or Mitley speaking like this to his betters.'

By this time one of the women had found a stool upon which to sit and she pulled out her knitting. The other ladies seeing this gave instructions to their children, or failing that, to any man foolish enough to catch their eye, to go fetch stools, chairs, settles and assorted other bum props and knitting, crochet, darning, embroidery or assorted fruits and vegetables for peeling and chopping.

'Jipple, don't forget to fill the kettle and put it over the fire!', shouted Gertie Griswold. Her tea was famous; she put the kettle on in the morning and placed some of her special super strong tea leaves into it and throughout the day as the water was either drunk or boiled away she continued to refill the kettle so that be the end of the day it was thick enough to caulk a boat.

'Oo, that sounds like a lovely idea. Here, Atty, go tell our Hulda to bring us out a nice cup of tea and a slice of bread and butter covered with the second best blackberry jelly, there's a dear.'

' LADIES WILL YOU PLEASE BE QUIET!' shouted Deeble.

'Well, why didn't you say that in the first place?' said Maisie.

'Yes, if you'd spoken with a bit of decorum in the first place there'd have been no cause for offence,' opined Gytha.

'Here, Gytha, de-cor-um that's a fine good word that is,' said Marge. I shall have to be remembering that for when my Cliff come home from the pub with 'that look' in his eye. You all knows the one don't you ladies?'

'Aye, 'that look' brought me seven children,' giggled Elsie. ' I put a stop to that when I learned to keep a long spoon by the side of the bed.'

'How did a spoon stop that then?' asked June who was one of the younger wives in the village.

'It were like being in the garden; every time the mole sticked his head above the ground I gave it a whack with me spoon. Bloody thing went down a lot faster than it came up I can tell ye!'

The old women all laughed while more than a few of the men looked at one another with the unspoken question: 'Does your missus do that too?'

Knowing the women were a force of nature able to withstand almost anything short of earthquake, war or a plague of locusts Deeble decided to retreat from the scene for a while.

THE PEN THIEF

by Lesley O'Brien

I am a hoarder of pens
I am the pen thief
They say it is mightier than the sword
I say it is a just and gallant cause!

LIBERTY IN CONFINEMENT

by Betsy Anderson

It's the middle of the night
I'm lying awake
My head's spinning
Gimme a break!
Lists, notes, plans, to do's
I try to shut it down
But I invariably lose
It's the early morning
I'm lying awake
The birds are singing
They've got nests to make
My head is calm
Still like a lake
I drift off to sleep
I should now be awake!

PLAYTIME

by Mandy O'Connor

"Can i go out and play yet, mum?"

COMPANION GARDENING

by Betsy Anderson

I thought I knew the garden like the back of my hand
The patches of earth, clay and sand
I thought I knew everything there was to know
what where when and how to sow
I even wrote a gardening blog: pictures of me gardening
In sun, in rain, in snow and in fog
Full of vibrant photos of flowers, foliage, fruit and veg
A few top tips, how to grow a prize winning hedge
I approached gardening with method and precision
What goes with what was a big decision
Dill and onions go well together
But when planted with tomatoes will cause them to wither
Companion planting: the key to success?
With a new interpretation, I'd have to say yes.

The garden was and is my haven
During lockdown it's been my salvation
Stay home, stay safe, hunker down and hide
A claustrophobic message, I need to get outside
The air is fresh, sun glistens on the dew
No distant hum as cars are few
The temperature is rising, warming my bones
Birds and bees fly above like inquisitive drones
Flowers, plants and trees hold their place
As squirrels dart amongst them, giving chase
Not just on Thursdays I can be heard clapping
To send the persistent wood pigeons flapping

A walk around the garden, coffee in hand
I'm like a troubadour, without a band
Drinking in colours with sheer delight
A new shoot is a wonderful sight
A plop from the pond catches my ear
I dart across to see what I hear
There he is our majestic bullfrog
A face to the resonant nightly monologue
Beside the pond shaded and guarded
Emerging spotted leaves foretell a wild orchid
I stand stock still as the blackbird takes a bath
I don't want to interrupt her, lest suffer her wrath

The trees are alive with a rainbow of birds
They communicate just fine, no need for words
Fluttering wings, A female Robin begs for food
Her mate obligingly responds, he's very good
This shows she can trust him when she's sitting on the eggs
To bring for her and her chicks, lots of daddy long legs
The nest boxes are a noisy hive of activity
In just a few weeks we'll herald the nativity
I suddenly realise this garden's not mine
We share it, it's ours and we get along just fine
As a conductor and orchestra, we play as one
As the songs of the garden resonate in the sun
Companion Planting is all very well
But Companion Gardening is where we excel.

THE CROFT

by Kate Trought

Rushing, gushing,
Silvery, tinkling, winkling
Shiny veined pebbles in the burn

From heather misted Highlands
Regal stag stands proud
Chiffon breath scrolling

Rustling, hustling
Amber gold and browned
Crinkling swooshing leaves

Breeze rising
Plumes fully bosomed of ptarmigan
Plumply feathered

Still, solid, granite cottage
Nestling, snuggling
Gazing through ochre illuminated eyes

SEEDS OF HOPE

by Margery Bambrick

Let's sew seeds of hope
Sow seeds of kindness
Seeds of compassion
Seeds of faith
Sew the seeds to plant and germinate
Seeds of nourishment
Seeds of encouragement
Sew the seeds of change
Change for the better, a better world

One where we can hold each other up, not be led by false truths,not be led by corporation but by co- operation

By people power in their wisdom, not people in power who's priority is power

Let's support our communities and allow them to care for each other, the environment and the land

Let's teach each other skills and knowledge

Let's pray together, meditate together, be together in our spiritual practise as a group and not led by ego

Lets love each other, lets heal each other, lets be healed

YOU WALK BESIDE ME

by Jules Drake

You Walk Beside Me
Less than a shadow
More than a dream
Real as the warmth of the sun
Untouched
Unseen

And when the darkness
Drags me down
You are my soul
Like the rising dawn

And when the dark
And the devil
Are done
You slip away

Less than a shadow
More than a dream

You Walk Beside Me

WISH

by Kate Trought

I wish you could

Tell me again that you love me
Tell me again that you care
Tell me again that you want me
Thread your fingers through my hair

Tell me again that you need me
Tell me and I'll be there
Put your arms out and just hold me
We always were a great pair

But I know

You're not here to tell me that you love me
You can't be by my side any more
That you didn't want to leave me
And you won't come back through the door

So

I'll sit right here with my memories
Kept warm by the love of my life
And be glad you were mine through the years dear
With me by your side as your wife

DILYS

by Kate Trought

You'll have heard of Dilys the Duck no doubt
Took millions of selfies perfecting her pout.
She plucked feather eyebrows and practised with lippy
Which didn't go well as her beak was too drippy.

She'd made the mistake of diving for food
Which turned out to be bread so didn't lighten her mood.
She shook her head wildly and gave a cross 'Quack!'
Her makeup all gone – and just for a snack.

She saw a dog walker her charge on a lead
So upended herself to graze in the weed
The spaniel barked loudly and started to dash
Into the water making a helluva splash

Dilys meantime was there underwater
Trying to find a bug she could slaughter
The first she knew of this shocking event
We're two soggy paws and their splashy descent

She popped up in alarm, her beak all a quiver
To see who had dared to jump in her river
The dog was quite happy snorting and shaking
And flapping its ears in the mud it was making

Dilys quite calm in this dire situation
Paddled in circles and quacked in frustration
The dog turned around and made for the bank
As its owner had given its lead a good yank.

The river stirred up by this furry intrusion
Continued to flow in spite of the confusion
The dog walker was laughing and pulled out her phone
Dilys cocked her head sideways and lowered her tone

The chance of a photo she couldn't resist
And all self publication was not to be missed
Her twirling and fluffing of feathers diminished
The huffing and puffing finally finished

'Good dog,' said the owner 'Now you sit right there,
While I get the light right and don't get a glare.
Look at you, Alfie, all soggy and silly
I'll take a quick photo before you get chilly.'

Dilys stopped circling and shrugged her brown feathers
Upended herself and showed off her nethers.

STILL BREATHING

by Ginny Britton

When you set out to let the birds free but the just fill the air above

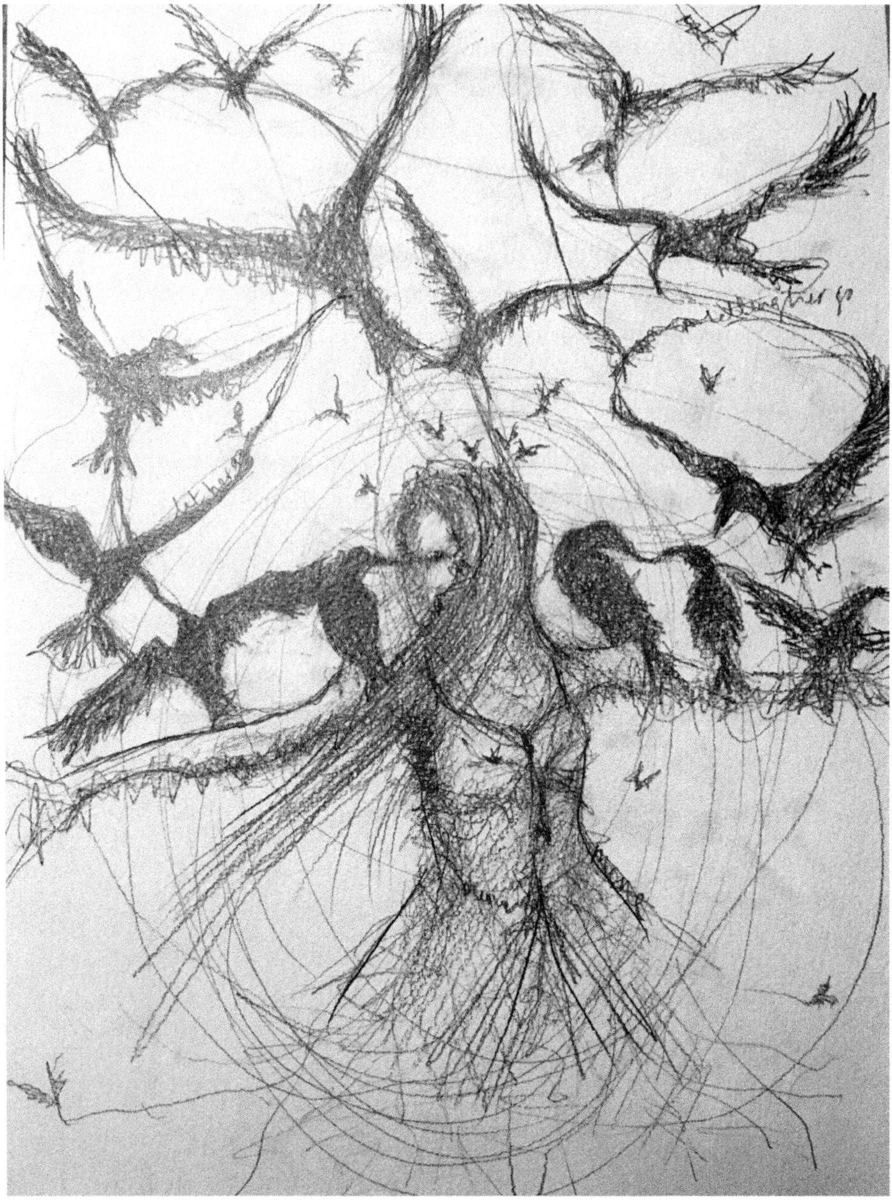

MANY HAPPY LOCKDOWNS

by Malcolm Scott

The letterbox rattles.

Just the four cards this year; a tangible manifestation of good wishes in this digital age.

Each one cheerfully celebrating the passing of another year; every one a continuum of my role in others' lives.

"Happy Birthday Brother/Dad/Husband/Nephew…"

There's no "Son" card this time round, a silent, nod to my father's passing last year, which brings me a moment of private reflection.

Fleeting, painful, blithe, by parts.

Amidst the lame jokes and awful puns, two cards contain the promise: "We'll celebrate properly when all this is over"; evoking a war-time message written by sons and lovers in hope-filled missives sent from unnamed locations.

The cards adorn the fireplace and I take them down and re-read the messages one last time. Their gaudy colours and cartoon images have brightened the living room this last week; catching the eye when I enter the room and diverting the mind from this grinding seclusion.

I think I'll keep them this year...before the strains of Paul Simon on the radio interrupt my reverie:

"Yesterday it was my birthday, I hung one more year on the line…" he proclaims, plaintively.

I grin. "Thanks Paul", I say out loud, and perfunctorily sing along to the end of the song.

"Age is just a state of mind", was one of the old man's favourite sayings. I file the cards away in the drawer and put the kettle on, and laugh once more at the recollection of one of his frequent sage musings on life.

Happy Birthday indeed.

A WONDERFUL DAY...

by Jacqui Stone

I connect with the Earth through my feet on the grass,
A wonderful day to watch the clouds pass.
The city is quiet, no-one rushing on by,
I sit here and watch just pondering why?

~

Why do we so often spend our lives on the run?
Why not take a break, spend some time in the sun?
Why not just watch, let the day gently unfold?
Why don't we slow down before we grow old?

~

A curious cat stops in its tracks,
It eyes me with interest then turns its back.
The pigeons and other birds come, and they go,
All nature around me just goes with the flow.

~

The trees so majestic reach up to the sky,
The blossom drifts down like snow from on high.
A bumblebee buzzes from flower to flower,
Blackbird sings his song, no matter the hour.

~

The wind ruffles my hair, I feel the sun on my face,
I let my eyes shut, drift away from this place.
I listen intently to the sounds all around,
The hum of the city keeps my feet on the ground.

~

But what if I dared to let my soul float away?
Leave my body right here, what would people say?
Head off on a journey, I've nothing to lose,
Where would I go, which soulscape would I choose?

~

Explore the silence of deserts, or rivers flowing wild,
An adventure in the mountains or forests loved as a child.
Or maybe the grasslands or oceans so deep,
My spirit guides for company and safety I keep.

~

Deeper and deeper and further I travel,
Time and space, it all starts to unravel.
The more I let go the more I feel free,
Reclaiming the real true essence of me.

~

The bark of a dog brings me back to this sphere,
How much time has passed whilst I've been sat here?
I feel rested, relaxed, blissful and calm,
Life didn't stop, no need for alarm.

~

I'm a wild wise warrior coming alive,
Taking time for myself and learning to thrive.
Connecting with nature, staying mindful as well,
Stimulating Stone with a story to tell...

THE MAGIC TRAVELLING WARDROBE

by Logan Stone (aged 10)

Due to the COVID 19 situation I was bored of being stuck in my immediate surroundings. I dreamt of the good old days, no restrictions, not as many rules and best of all being able to see my friends. But luckily Bo Jo does not know about my travelling wardrobe. It is in my Dad's bedroom because I only have a chest of drawers and I don't even think he knows it can take you places.

On the first misty morning of May I realised that I needed a change of scenery, so I invited my friends to the beach for a meetup. I tentatively entered the wardrobe. Pushing past my Dad's shirts I fall through the end as I trip over a discarded coat hanger. Luckily the landing is not what I expected as I land on a soft sandy beach. The first thing that hits me is the smell of the salty sea air rolling in off the waves.

"As the one who invited you all here, I would like to offer some refreshments and an assortment of games" I say. The children's excitement was immeasurable, and the sound of their laughter was great to hear.

Then they all said in unison, "I can't believe we are out of lockdown early."

As all the others were playing, I decided to join in but as a game called Nubbel ended, a small fight started but it was easily resolved, they just had a re-match.

It felt amazing and I never wanted it to end, but then I hear a distant shouting. I wake up and I realise it was just a dream and that I still have to do home-schooling (boo).

The End

ABC~OVID-19

by May Halyburton

AAAAAAAAAAAAAAAGH!

BLEEPING COVID DISEASE!

Everyone Fearing Germs!

HORRID!

Isolation Justified.....

Kisses lost,

masks now on.

People queuing...rationing supplies,

TENSE,

(understandably)

VALUE WASHING!!!!!

WASH WASH WASH

? ? ?

Xmas....

YOURSELF?

ZERO-CONTACT!!!

AAAAAAAAAAAAAAAGH!

LETTING GO

by Ginny Britton

Often when we hold ourselves in and all the baggage that is us, it takes just 4 words from someone who we trust and that actually see's us to set it free.

" Just let it go...."

"Sometimes that's harder than that simple sentence" I said.

" Okay, then draw it"

So I did. And this is it. Letting everything go, right out of my chest and onto paper.

Raw and true.....

COVID-19

by Elisabeth Fraser-Jackson

Everything looks the same,
as it has always been
But lurking in the shadows,
is the thing that's never seen.

Watching and waiting until you
make a mistake,
Then it wraps its arms around you,
your body it does take.

Why is it here,
what purpose does it serve,
Destroying lives in its wake,
its vastness does unnerve.

Aside from the damage,
its legacy does leave,
Was there a hidden message of
what it would achieve.

New ways of working,
no longer nine to five,
People recognising what's
important to survive.

Communities pulling together,
finding long lost ways,
To love and support each other
throughout the COVID haze.

Nature is renewing, no longer
feeling threatened,
Foxes, deer and dolphins too
praising what has lessened.

Despite all the heartache COVID 19
has surely caused,
We can all love one another,
despite our human flaws.

So when all this is over,
let's hope some things remain,
We are kinder to each other and
value our domain.

MANHATTAN MOMENT

by Dawne Kovan

Late autumn raining in Manhattan. The rain leaches and cuts buildings down to size. I'm sitting in Barnes and Noble on Third Avenue, as I do each morning. I drink coffee and watch New Yorkers.

I know few people, yet, and have even fewer landmarks to measure by. I don't even know if this is a storm or a shower – how can I judge how long I might be sitting here? I have books to browse. It's people I'm browsing now. The books sit on the on the table.

"Excuse me." She wants to share my table. I move my books to one side. She smiles and puts her hot chocolate down. The smell swirls between us. I recognise her. Over the last couple of days I have seen her walking. Her presence connects me to this place. I live in a neighbourhood. People here do regular things and I am part of it.

Across the street a group of office workers stand together beneath the canopy of their doorway. They gossip; they flick their cigarettes

"Such a disgusting habit – they shouldn't even be allowed to smoke in the street," the woman comments, without looking at me.

"Back home - in London - people smoke openly everywhere, all the time," I tell her. She looks shocked. A bus swishes uptown, wipers working, tyres send water out in all directions.. Now the office workers have disappeared – despite the damp air a pall of smoke remains.

The weather has set in. Time to be on my way. In the doorway I try to work out how best to get back to my apartment on the lower East Side. The downtown buses go south down Second Avenue on the east and Lexington on the west. I decide on Lexington. It's a prettier ride. I want to see the Chrysler Building, even in the rain.

The rank sea and river water wafts on the wind. The bus rolls carefully as if not to engulf me with the flood at my feet.

"Good morning ma'am – how are you?" asks the bus driver, as I step up.

"Wet."

He grins and closes the storm outside. I sit behind.

Just as we begin to move off, he slams on the brakes.

"Hey!" shouts a man behind me.

The driver grunts "Sorry".

A woman on the sidewalk bangs her fist on my window.

"Damned bus drivers," she mouths at me. I shrug. The driver sighs and stands. And steps down onto the sidewalk. Wind whips through the doors; I draw my jacket close.

"Probably a drunk. Did we hit him? Did anyone see?"

The driver clambers back.

"We can't move until the ambulance takes this ass-hole to hospital," he informs us. "The cops will probably want witness statements. Meantime, folks, no one moves."

New Yorkers love a spectacle. Maybe a TV news crew will come and interview us. A woman, dressed in New York black, raincoat, natty boots, checks her hair in the window. She's probably heading down to Gramercy Park for a smart lunch. She produces a red lipstick and applies it to her mouth. Pressing her lips together, she sees me watching: " You never know," she says.

Now the rain obscures my view. Sirens wail towards us, but I can't tell yet which emergency service it is. An ambulance whoops and stops right next to me. I can see more clearly. Cars hoot and brake to make some cryptic point. Everyone leans for a better view. As if we're girls together, the smart woman sits beside me and squeezes my arm.

Paramedics jump out of the ambulance and carry apparatus around the front of the bus. They bring out a stretcher.

"Someone's hurt bad," says a passenger.

"I didn't hit nobody," insists the driver, eyes towards me.

The paramedics seem to be carrying a bundle of old rags towards the rear of the ambulance. The tramp's eyes are closed and he's unconscious. Now I'm sorry for him. He opens his eyes, grins at me, then winks.

"I guess he'll sit the storm out warm in the hospital," the smart woman says.

The ambulance pulls away.

The bus driver tells us. "These winos lie in the road and wait."

"And we wait," the smart woman says. "Nothing happens. It's awful."

Two cop cars glide away.

The driver says "It's all over folks - let's go"

A LONG AWAITED FRIENDSHIP

by May Halyburton

I made a new friend today. She reminded me of someone. She has a quiet demeanour but is a conscientious, non-judgemental listener. I felt safe as she accompanied me, whilst observing the two metre social distancing rule. So much in common. She followed me home. I invited her in.

LOCKDOWN ZOO

by Elisabeth Fraser-Jackson

My eyes flew open, my heart somersaulting in my chest and perspiration trickling down in droplets. Is this it, the "thing" COVID -19? No, it's a nightmare! Eyes, big staring eyes watching and waiting. They say your dreams tell you something so what was this dream saying to me? Ahh, now I remember. All those messages - wash your hands, don't touch your face, don't rub your eyes. Eyes - brown, blue, green and every colour in between eyes. Those all seeing eyes. Usually told to protect those eyes for sight, now there is a greater need to protect them from the "thing". It has an entry point! Am I going mad, is this all a dream? Buddhists believe life is an illusion, I hope they're right!

My mind racing, I get up. I need to write to tame my mind. Some Buddhist monks call it taming the tiger or calming the monkey and some psychiatrists call it your chimp. Well I can tell you my tiger, monkey or chimp are going ballistic! I start to laugh remembering an old boss saying "throw the monkeys out of your backpack"! The mind conjures up images of chattering monkeys flying through the air trying to find trees to cling on to. If only it were that simple to clear the mind huh! The mind , a wonderful tool but also a flighty piece of nonsense. My mind all over the place since the "thing" decided to invade our lives. Perceived mixed messages from government and police invading my thought processes and causing confusion.

I should walk, walk in the hills that calms my mind. Oh wait - is that ok? I have to drive. Is that classed as essential travel? Well, it's essential to tame my tiger, monkey or chimp. I recall the minister on the television saying it was ok to drive a short distance to walk in isolation. Oh wait! What was that message on Facebook last night? The police are stopping people driving for a walk and sending them home. Could I pretend I'm going shopping? Pretend, just listen to yourself PRETEND, your mum wouldn't like that. She taught you honestly was the best policy. She also said you were no good at telling lies! I told you my tiger, monkey or chimp were going crazy and I'm only at the start of lockdown.

They are asking we more vulnerable souls to stay in for 12 weeks. Now before some cheeky sod says it, I'm not over 70 but OMG if I don't calm my tiger, monkey or chimp, I will look like I'm 70! Suffering from asthma classes me as vulnerable. Vulnerable moi! I like to think I can kick anyone's ass! Oh wait, it's not ANYONE, it's the "thing"! Does it even have an ass to kick? Do I have to remind you again that my tiger, monkey and chimp are in overdrive?

Now that a walk in the hills seems to be out of the question, I best meditate. I've been taught meditation by Buddhists so no need for guided meditation. I just sit and stare into space and follow the breath. What's that? Would someone tell my tiger, monkey or chimp to shut up! Anyone recommend some good, soothing guided meditation?

ROLE MODEL

by Mandy O'Connor

"When that milk is gone! It'll be gone" I screech. I'm already at volume 10 and it's barely past eight O clock. I struggle to watch them pour this white gold over cereal as if the cheerios are thirsty. What if the shops run out. 'Pandemic-shamdemic' is the look they throw me.

I was calm yesterday when a whole roll of toilet paper was massacred for a game of 'floor is lava'. I oblivious, as they Perforated each precious square and distributed it all over the house. Tell that story to the lady I almost knocked down and killed in a Lidl car park. Why, because the mountainous pile of loo roll she was grasping covered her face as she was blown in front of my car.

But what kind of role model am I being at this time of crisis? I know I should be saying "let's just eat toast for breakfast" if the milk runs dry, or "let's find a bag for all this loo roll, you silly sausages", I am however still allowed to scream "stupid cow" at the supermarket woman because I was alone in the car that day. See, I'm great at modelling social distancing. But, I don't always do that. I shout. I yell sometimes.

As parents, we do what we can and always hope tomorrow will be a better day or as my dad would say "don't let the b'stards grind you down". I should add, he's not specifically referring to my children here.

ONE FOR SORROW

by Malcolm Scott

4:30 a.m. I open the back door and pad silently to the garden shed; my refuge where I used to go to self-isolate in pre-isolation days.

I'd followed the advice of the stream of talking heads who'd advised me to "de-clutter your home, de-clutter your mind", by starting with my home from home, and had spent the best part of all of yesterday clearing it out.

I'm therefore strangely cheered by the sight of paint cans all neatly stacked and the garden tools hung uniformly on hooks. The freshly swept floor is now clear of debris and I sit down on the beaten-up armchair; the one piece of furniture redeemed from the pile destined for the tip.

I turn the radio on and the plummy tones of the Radio 4 presenter relaying the baleful update of the number of Corona virus victims dampens my optimistic mood, and I quickly turn it back off.

I welcome the silence, but presently the air is punctuated by the "chook-chook" call of a nosey blackbird who has alighted on the ground just outside the open shed door.

He edges closer as I tempt him with a strand of dough torn from my bread roll and noisily devours it not two feet from me; his hunger temporarily overcoming his natural caution in sharing my space.

He is quickly joined by his mate, their audible presence now in stereo and increasing in volume as they seem to harangue me for more scraps; there's a portentous air to their trilling now... like Poe's raven they lecture me in a disapproving tone; brow-beating me, snaring me in my wooden box.

5:10 a.m. I turn the radio on again, just in time for the God slot. The beguiling words of the presenter assures me that "redemption from this plague can be found through the medium of prayer", and proceeds to offer up her own soliloquy to a higher power.

The early hour and stillness add certain potency to her address; her words resonate; my synapses quarrel, but cynicism ultimately wins the day.

I sit back in my rickety chair; the warm tea settling in my stomach makes me drowsy, and I nap, fitfully.

6: a.m. The pips signalling the news bulletin wakes me from my slumber. The body count rises once more; an unrelenting litany of gloom and despair, briefly interrupted by talk of lifting of restrictions of movement, but the sense of a society imploding prevails.

I close the shed door, and my friend the blackbird perches on the fence nearby. I present my hands in an open fashion to him, plaintively telling him that I have no more bread; he squawks in disgust and flies back to his nest, and I turn on my heel and walk back to mine.

GUILT

by Julia Cochrane

While countries are in lockdown
and the world is grieving
I'm at home with my children
drawing, painting, playing and building

I get to watch my kids grow and blossom
to show them how exciting our garden can be
I get to paint beautiful rainbows to put in our windows
and read them stories and show them how to be free

I have the privilege of exploring their world
of living in their wonderful imagination
I have been a pirate, a shark, a dragon, a t-rex
I have worn pants on my head with no explanation

I am laughing, I am fun, I feel happy
I am tired, I am anxious, I feel guilty
Guilty for laughing and playing
when this time is dark for so many

But it is also precious and should be treasured
without guilt or fear of being measured
It's ok to see the light and feel the sun
It's ok to smile and have lots of fun.

CUPPA?

by Mandy O'Connor

I would take up his offer of a cup of tea if only I could be certain that he wouldn't spit it in first. Yes. Things have become that bad. It's hard to remember a time when we were in love. At first, there was lust, fun but I doubt a real connection. Didn't stop us having three kids together though. Oops.

We were scheduled to marry on the 21st of March of this year. We finally decided to call it off after the Band, caterers, best man and all of the groom's family cancelled and the small matter of an uncontrollable virus. The self obsessed part of my personality wonders if this pandemic is a sign. Thousands of people dying to prevent me from making a huge mistake. After the Madrid bombings in 2004, my flatmate decided to quit our course "Life's too short to be miserable" she said as she packed for Italy. Nice sentiment, babe but who's taking over your room?

So, I've decided to drink through this Lock down. Probably not the best embellishment for my personality but... Hungover or not, I wake each morning at 6.30am, pull on spandex and run for three miles. Seems as if all the dogs walked at this hour have behavioral problems. I guess I am in good company,

ISOLATIONIST IN ISOLATION
by Abigail Kirkpatrick

Everyone has been talking and discussing this virus. I want to relate and contribute my experience but alas do I truly have anything to contribute?

My days have not changed, my nights remain as turbulent as always and my thoughts and worries always keep my mind from sleeping.

The outside world has always seemed scary. Full of people whose actions and behaviour is impossible to predict.

Staying indoors has and is my life, these walls I have built around myself like a cage of my own making.

Others are stressed and fearful of the coming days, myself included but what can I do? what can I say?

All I can do is repeat my endless cycle. Keep myself from the negative thoughts and wait but maybe for once I don't feel so alone.

TIME

by Mandy O'Connor

'A watch doesn't require hands when a man has no where to go'

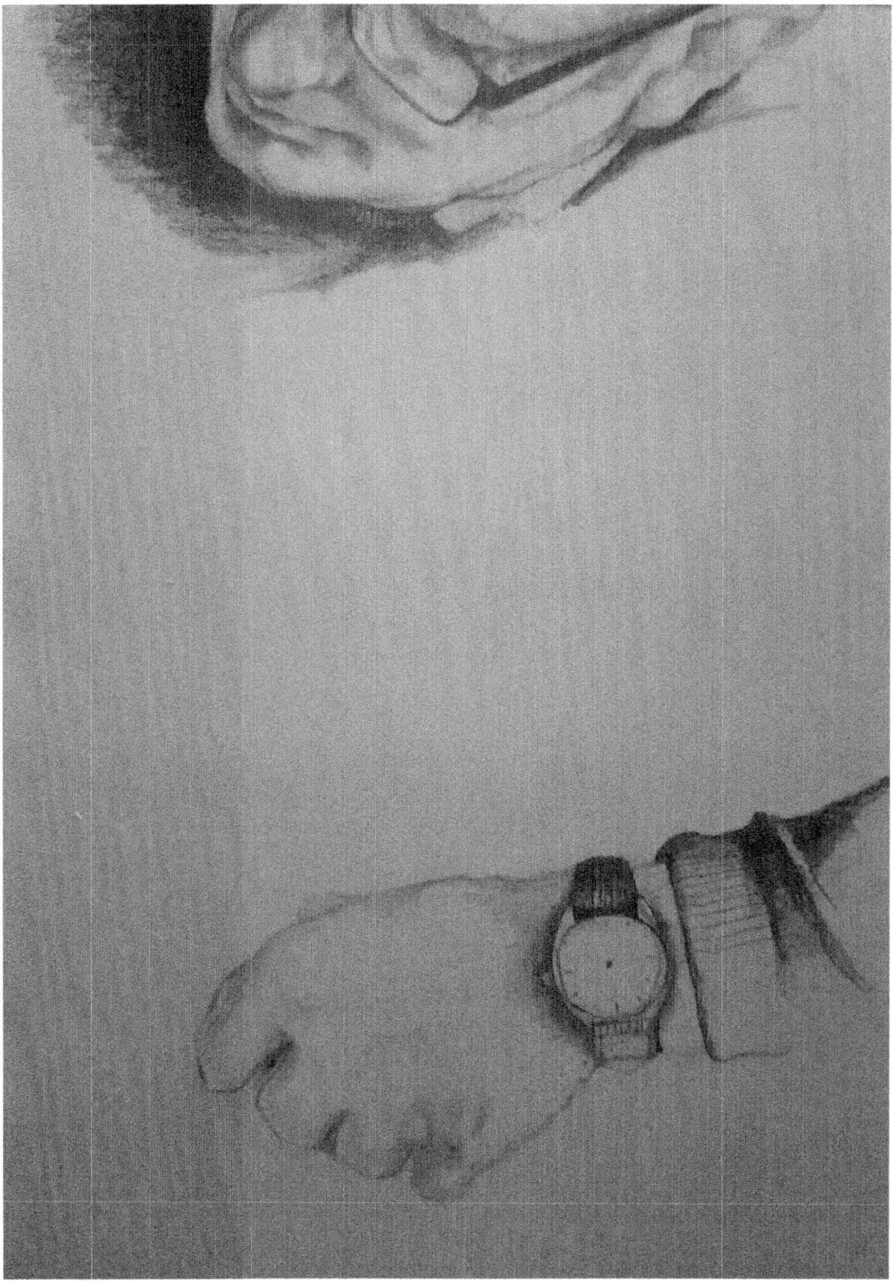

OWNERSHIP

by Ginny Britton

Taking control of what has always ruled you and learning how to navigate that.

SALAD DAYS - GARDENING IN A TIME OF VIRUS

by Liza Miles

The clay under the turf resists the fork,
Not wanting to be broken and shine light
Into the earthworms home.
A flash of pink slips away to hide once more.

The roots from plants of the past gardener
whose hands shaped this bed of potential.
There are secrets in this sod,
Where wanton weeds and wildflowers grow.

And who am I to think I can change the plan,
Whose time is long past her salad days
Yet wants to plant salad
to feast on and delight in the years left.

And in future days my salad will be redug
by younger hands with lithe limbs to tend it
And I will not cry
My heart felt planting will bloom beyond this virus..

MAGICAL WORDS

by Katerina Dufkova

Dedicated to Pete

So you said the magical words.

How can three little words mean so much?

The feeling,which started at the top of my head, feels like a liquid sunshine running through my veins.

The only thing it compares to is the feeling of being held in your arms, my head nestled in the curve of your shoulder, feeling you close and listening to your beautiful voice as you talk about our next adventures.

I can taste the smile on your lips when you lean down to kiss me.

The three simple words that are making me feel like I can fly and in that moment I wish I could.

I would fly to you, to the place where I feel safe and loved and excited.

To the place where I could trace that smile on your face, blindly.

To the place where days are not bleeding into one and where compassion and care live.

I would fly over the locked-down houses, full of stir-crazy hearts.

Hearts that yearn to be seen and heard and held.

Perhaps if I could fly to you, I would rain some of the feeling your words have started into those stir-crazy hearts so they could feel a bit more peaceful.

So, from the bottom of my stir crazy heart, thank you for finding the courage to say the three magical words.

I

Love

You

SEEKING HUMANITY

by Lesley O'Brien

Inside me a giant question mark, a mark of questions
heaps and heaps that grow like mushrooms in a dingy cellar
til someone unlocks the door and they fall, stumble out
crush me with their querying looks. Answers, I want answers they shout!

Questions with answers that breed lies
like Hill Billy's on a mountain top, thundering lies
I don't want to hear them, I want the homespun
songs and stories of the old ones.

Nostalgia in their eyes, tears clogging their throats
with love stuck on the inside looking for a vent
lives built with honesty and knowledge that is certain
we borrow the earth from our children.

Inside me a tiny seed, a seed of humanity
that seeks the light of day, a friendly face,
willing to embrace the quiver of a note
that will pierce my heart with the wisdom of truth.

TAMING THE HOUND

by Liza Miles

Agnes turned over, she couldn't face the day quite yet.

Below her the neighbours dog was crying, barking, kicking up a fuss.

"**C**ody, be quiet," Agnes whispered under her breath.

Damn it, the dog was loud enough to wake the whole neighbourhood.

Eilidh should be home from night shift by now, surely?

From outside the window she could hear the dawn chorus.

Groaning, her body aching from a disturbed night, Agnes's concern about Cody's distress forced her to get up.

"**H**elp, help me." the voice was faint but definitely Eilidh's.

"**I**'m coming," Agnes called, throwing on her dressing gown and flip flops.

"**J**eepers, what on earth happened ..." Agnes' words were out before she could stop herself as she saw her neighbour prostrate on the ground beside her van.

Knowing first aid well she knew she could not move Eilidh, and wondered about the rules for emergency close contact during Covid.

"**L**ook I'm going to call for an ambulance, I'll be quick grabbing my phone" Ages cursed herself for not bringing it down with her.

"**M**mmm," Eilidh groaned, it's a good sign she's conscious and can understand what's going on, Agnes thought.

"**N**ine, nine, nine" Agnes muttered to herself, she had just moved back from Canada and emergency there was 911.

"**O**h thank goodness, they're almost here" Agnes whispered to Eilidh as they heard the sirens.

"**P**lease, Cody ... " Eilidh's voice was faint and Cody had not stopped barking and crying from inside the house.

"**Q**uite ok," said Agnes, "we'll take care of him."

"**R**ight oh," said the paramedic, "she'll be at forth valley for the next day or so at least."

“**S**hould I follow you …” Agnes hesitated, fearful of what going to the hospital might mean for her and her family.

“**T**hat’s not allowed right now, sorry,” replied the paramedic.

“**U**nderstood,” Agnes breathed a sigh of relief.

Vanquishing her personal fears about Cody, a stressed mixed breed rescue, Agnes went into Eilidh’s flat.

“**W**hat’s up Cody, is your mistress ill?”

Xenodogphobic, her daughter had once described her, when she admitted to not liking certain dog breeds, or large dogs that looked fierce, very much like Cody.

“**Y**ou’re a good boy really,” said Agnes softly, hoping to win the brute round holding out her hand with the crunchy morsels..

Zipping closed the bag of treats Eilidh had motioned for her to take before she was loaded into the ambulance, Agnes sighed with relief, “Well done me, job done, now where’s the fucking wine?”

THE LAST SUNSET OF 2019

by May Halyburton

The fiery, iridescent ball seemed reluctant to set. Its radiance strained as it desperately clutched at the horizon in vain. The palm trees bowed reverently and the sea silenced her agitated waves in respect. The decade was done.

We celebrated, making resolutions in blissful ignorance.

LEADER WANTED

by Liza Miles

There was once a leader called Boras
Who was really a horrible Horace
He rambled and muttered
His ideas totally cluttered
Churchilllian ambitions up my arse.

A GIFT TO MYSELF

by Shusha Lamoon

The stillness, the calm, the peace ... is gone.

The normal, the mundane, the humdrum ... is gone.

However, hard I try I cannot grasp them, they're gone, slipping through my fingers like a mist, there but not there.

There is silence in isolation but not quiet. Not even in the dead of night.

Whirring, churning, tossing and turning endless possibilities, alternatives, outcomes.

My mind now constantly alert, confronting my fears, hunting for solutions that don't exist, searching for safety, which eludes me.

And so this is the new "normal" ... I crave the old. I wish I could take it back. Say sorry for taking it for granted. Not appreciating it. Not realising what I had, when I had it.

Because if I could get it back, I would grasp it with both hands and never let it go. Instead of spending years ... years searching for happiness, I could have been content with the ordinary. What a gift! Contentedness.

When this is all over, this is what I am going to gift to myself – a lifetime of contentedness with the ordinary, humdrum, mundaneness of life. What a joy!

WOEBEGONE DAYS

by Malcolm Scott

Occasioning sadness
Wading thru' the madness
Bound up, iron clad
No joy at feeling sad.

Pessimism, misery,
Stay safe, keep alert
Save lives, Victory!
Socially distance, disconnect.

Worry beads and talisman,
Whisky in a hip flask;
Totem poles and keepsakes
Newton's cradle click-clacks.

Gossiping and chattering,
Shortages and rationing
Nostalgia overload
and manufactured panicking.

Late night coffee with
Peace of mind elusive;
Unanswered invocations
Anxiety, intrusive ...

THE UNWELCOME VISITOR

by Toni Thomson

My mum says not to worry
To make sure and wash my hands
There's a germ that's very nasty
That's crossing lots of lands.

My Dad says it's okay
As long as we are strong.
We have to be more cautious
Hopefully, not for long.

My teacher said school's closing
She will send me lots of tasks
I've just to try and do my best
And that is all she asks.

My friends all say that they're fed up
We can't meet up to play
We wave and smile through windows
As we go for a walk each day.

My sister says she likes it.
She's happy stuck at home
Doing lots of things together
But I sometimes feel alone.

My Grandma says to FaceTime
And drags in Grandpa too
We check up on each other
Because that's what families do.

My neighbour shouts hello and waves
When we stand outside to clap
Thanking all those people working
Every woman and every chap.

My TV tells me it's still not safe
We need to isolate.
We have to carry on this way
Stay home, stay safe and wait.

Nobody tells me about the deaths
But I know and it's really bad
I hear them talking quietly
I feel immensely sad.

I say one day we'll beat it
This evil germ unseen
That's created carnage in my world
Go away COVID19!

We all ask when it's over
Will things ever be the same?
Who knows, but we will be prepared
In case it comes again!

CORONACATION

by Liza Miles

My neighbours are having a “coronacation”
And they’re doing it in style.

Tents up in the garden, barbecue and a fire
Well why not! Cheers to them, I smile.

Ooh how comfy, now she’s lying on an air mattress, legs akimbo,
Sure trumps my towel, old and torn, I won it free at bingo.

A bottle of beer a cup of tea a glass or two of gin
Beats my day working from home and peering out from within

Ah, three O clock, time to say done, shut this baby down
My turn now for outside fun, turn that envious frown upside down

THE CLOUD LOVE

by Esther Idowu

I watch the clouds go by
I see them fade into the blue sky
Moment by moment the fluff goes by
As the colour changes right in my eyes

I watch the cloud go by
From grey to white under the blue sky
To let the shine make its way through
Bringing delights to my heart

I watch the clouds go by
Each fluffy flakes adds beauty to the sky
Moving so gently to merge into one
To look like a sugar candy sweet on my tongue

I watch the clouds go by
And it brings desire close by
For the sky is blue and my love is true
And each new day brings me joy to bloom.

I am Fortunate
I am Esther Abiola
Delightedly loving seeing the cloud go by.

Printed in Great Britain
by Amazon

40501346R00061